The Empire of Sleep

The Empire of Sleep

Henri-Frédéric Blanc

Translated from the French by Nina Rootes

Secker & Warburg LONDON

Originally published in France
as *L'Empire du sommeil* © Actes Sud, 1989

This edition first published in England 1992
by Martin Secker & Warburg Limited
Michelin House, 81 Fulham Road, London SW3 6RB

Translation copyright © 1992 by Secker & Warburg

With many thanks to Carys and Jean-Ives Le Disez.

Set in Century Old Style, 11 on 14¼ point
by Deltatype Ltd, Ellesmere Port
Printed in Great Britain
by St Edmundsbury Press, Bury St Edmunds, Suffolk

To sleep is to return home.

Old Chinese proverb

Part One

Joseph took a great gulp of fresh air. A church clock struck eleven, or perhaps it was midnight. At that moment, the full October moon appeared from behind the yellow clouds. On the corners of the deserted streets, the lamplight shone on the piles of rubbish. Somewhere in the depths of the city, a drunkard was shouting. Joseph stopped in front of a heap of dead leaves, selected a particularly beautiful one for his cat and put it into his medical bag. It was starting to rain again and, naturally, he had again left his umbrella somewhere. He made his way towards the metro entrance.

Waiting on the platform, he thought about the house-call he had just made. 'That woman,' he said to himself, 'was really the bloody limit. First, she begs me to come because she can't sleep, then, when I arrive, she calls me every name under the sun because I've woken her up . . . Well, that settles it, from now on, no more house-calls, *basta*! Some people panic because it takes them ages to get to sleep, some call me in to relate some nightmare, others hold a knife to my throat and demand an instant diagnosis of all their problems, and others again want me to poison them with soporific drugs. Playing the sandman to all these neurotics is beginning to get on my tits. Either they ignore what I say because they've lost faith in everything, or they hang on my every word as if I were the Messiah . . . No doubt about it, the future belongs to the shrinks.'

The train came in. Joseph got into an empty carriage, yawned fit to crack his jaws and lounged back voluptuously, happy in the thought that he would soon be tucked up in bed.

At the next station, four young people got in, three girls and a boy. They had obviously just come from a fancy-dress ball. The young girls, with their dishevelled hair, their white-powdered faces and blood-red lips, were dressed as punk witches. There were rents in their black tights, revealing glimpses of creamy skin. They appeared to be naked under their studded leather jackets. The boy was got up as a devil: goatee beard, red cape and forked tail. He was incredibly good-looking. He started fooling about to amuse the girls, whispering into their ears, sliding his hands up under their jackets and tickling them, while they laughed and played with his devil's tail.

They had not yet noticed Joseph, who was watching them in fascination. What wouldn't he have given to be that boy, to be twenty years younger! He would willingly have chucked everything onto the fire – all his labour, all his research – for the chance to dance with those girls, nibble their necks, get drunk on the smell of their flesh, bury his nose in their masses of curly hair. Youth . . . after all, he deserved it far more than they did. For countless nights, he had studied and meditated, ruined his eyesight scribbling page after page, knocked his brains out in the hope of finding buried gold in his grey matter. Result: his only dream, nowadays, was to be able to stop thinking, to enjoy life like an animal. He should have known better: intelligence is non-returnable, consciousness irreversible. We have the capacity to learn, but not the power to forget what we know. While he had been searching for ambrosia in his brain, his life had taken on the taste of stale porridge. His ideas had led him to nothing but more ideas. And the more he learned about things, the more he was afflicted with doubts.

'A coward,' he said to himself, 'that's what I am. Opening a book is easier than living. With your nose in a book, you're not exposing yourself to any risks. You're king of the castle. But those young people have got the right idea. They laugh, they enjoy themselves, they live without asking themselves what life is all about.'

And he looked at them, hypnotised by their freshness and their young, cat-like agility, while he himself felt as if he weighed several tons.

Suddenly the boy shouted, 'Where is everybody? The devil needs an audience . . . Aha! I spy someone . . . a more or less human being . . .'

He came up to Joseph and bent over him. Black eyes sparkled in an angelic face.

'How much?' he asked.

'How much what?' Joseph answered, startled by the question.

'Your soul. How much?'

Joseph smiled. 'I'd have a job giving it to you,' he said, 'I wouldn't know where to start looking.'

'You don't have to give it to me,' said the boy, 'just let me take it for myself. I'm sure it's no earthly use to you.'

'Quite right, and it would be nothing but a nuisance to you.'

'A second-hand soul, shrivelled up and self-doubting . . . hmm, not worth a lot, is it? I'll give you . . . let's say, a colour telly. How'd you like that, eh? It'll help you get through whatever time you've got left.'

'I never watch television,' Joseph replied.

'Ah, that's tricky . . . How about a lawn-mower? Keep you busy on Sundays?'

'I don't have a garden.'

'Well then, what would you say to a deep-freeze? There's a useful thing now! You've always got something you can freeze.'

The girls were giggling. Joseph started laughing, too.

'There's no room in my kitchen,' he said.

'Let's see then, what would really give you pleasure?' the boy asked, stroking his little pointed beard. 'What do you do?'

'Actually, I'm a doctor. Or rather, a researcher. Yes, that's more exact because I spend more time . . .'

'A researcher! I should have guessed, you look the very image of a man who's always racking his brains. So, that's it, you do research . . . you seek . . . and I bet you haven't found, eh? Oh

5

dear, oh dearie me! I really am too hard on scientists, and yet, do you know, hell would have no future without them. Once upon a time, if you wanted to spread a false idea, it was a hell of a job, and you had to traipse off on the most boring old travels. Nowadays, thanks to science, the lie flourishes, it spreads much faster and, thanks to technology and progress, eventually it gets diffused all over the world! Well, Mr Researcher, how would you like to find what you're looking for? All I ask in exchange is your soul. Come on, let's make it a deal, OK? Right, done!'

Adroitly, he ripped an advertisement for a bank out of one of the panels, then took a pen from his pocket and wrote on the back of it:

> *I the undersigned declare that I surrender my soul to the Great Billy-Goat, the Prince of this World, in return for which the aforesaid guarantees me outstanding success in my work.*

'There!' he said, 'I've made out the standard contract for you. All you have to do is sign at the bottom.'

The girls were hysterical with laughter. The boy held out the pen and paper. Joseph, not wanting to look like an old square, took them and signed.

'*Grazie molto!*' said the boy, snatching back paper and pen. Then he went back to the girls, who were devouring him with their eyes.

'There we are!' he said, 'Simple as picking your nose! In fact, it's getting easier and easier. Soon, they'll be queueing up to sign. In the old days, if you wanted to catch a soul, you had to get up very early in the morning and go through your whole bag of tricks. Now, you don't even have to wear a disguise! Just wait till I tell the boys *down below* about this, they'll never believe me!'

Joseph said to himself: 'It's really a pleasure to see young people who still have a sense of humour and haven't succumbed to the general gloom.'

The train stopped at the Temple station. As Joseph opened the door, the boy called out 'Goodnight, Mr Researcher! And don't scratch your brains too hard, you might make a hole in them!'

Joseph got out, to a chorus of laughter from the girls. He turned back to watch the train disappearing into the tunnel. In the carriage, he could see the boy pulling a mock-sorrowful face and waving goodbye with his tail.

The rain was letting up. Joseph no longer felt sleepy. He felt wide-awake and fighting fit. Seeing those kids had really given him a lift. He tried to do an *entrechat* and almost came a cropper on some dog-shit.

At the door of the house where he lived, he stopped to polish the brass plate with his sleeve:

DOCTOR JOSEPH CAVALCANTI
Diseases and disorders of sleep

Then he pushed open the heavy front door and climbed the stairs that reeked of stale cat-piss. He lived at the top, on the third floor. The only bulb still working was on the ground floor and, as usual, he had to grope his way up the last flight.

He opened the door of his flat and turned on the light in the hall. He took off his raincoat, promising himself for the umpteenth time to have it cleaned as soon as the weather improved, and hung it gingerly on the hat-stand, which was so riddled with woodworm that it threatened to collapse at any moment.

Livingstone, his venerable alley-cat, was comfortably installed on the battered and dusty volumes of Jules Verne's *Voyages extraordinaires*. The cat yawned grandiloquently, jumped down on to the carpet and, rubbing his master's legs as he passed, made his way resolutely, but without haste, to the kitchen. Joseph followed him, poured some milk into his bowl and decided to make himself some coffee. For once, he felt like writing.

Minutes later, with a cup of coffee in his hand, he surveyed his library, which also served as his bedroom and which he called his 'dreamery'. There were two windows, one overlooking the street and the other the inner courtyard of the building. They were hung with heavy scarlet curtains. Beside a bulky leather armchair, scored and striped with claw marks, stood his desk, an old oak table cluttered with books and papers, a bronze bust of Napoleon and a framed photograph, already fading, which had been taken during his national service. It showed Joseph standing in front of a tank.

On the opposite side of the room, between the window that gave on to the street and a wardrobe with a mirror on the door, was his 'work bed'. It was covered with a red eiderdown and above it hung a large portrait of Christopher Columbus surrounded by African masks.

Everywhere there were books, books and more books, piling up like the years.

The cat came in, licking his chops, settled himself in the middle of a maze of old tomes and started his ablutions. Joseph took the dead leaf out of his medical bag and threw it to him. Livingstone sniffed at it suspiciously for a long time, then, reassured, he pounced on it, rolled his eyes like a cat possessed and began furiously tearing it to pieces.

The telephone rang. It was Léger, a crusty, fire-eating librarian with whom Joseph had made friends several years earlier during an auction of antiquarian books.

'What a beautiful night, O great wizard of dreams and juggler of comets! I hope I haven't woken you up? I know you go to bed late
. . .'

'As a matter of fact,' Joseph replied, 'I was just getting ready to do some work.'

'Ah. And that famous treatise of yours, the essay on sleep, how's it coming along?'

'Ugh . . . I keep asking myself what earthly use it is, writing
. . .'

'None whatsoever, dear boy. But the Himalayas are no use either. Nevertheless, you get a bloody marvellous view from the

8

summit! Asking yourself what use it is means you're already poking your finger into the degrading and destructive gear-wheels of universal money-grubbing. One must serve truth, not ask oneself what use it is. Maybe you'll gain nothing by it, but at least you'll avoid self-disgust and boredom. So, get on with it, O great sleeper, and write! The only hard part is getting that first word down on paper! By the way, I rang up because I've got something for you. I'm keeping it as a surprise. Drop into the library one evening, I never close before eight o'clock.'

'OK, I'll look in.'

'Well, keep your pecker up, good luck with the work and may gentle zephyrs fan your sleep! And don't forget to sleep with all sail spread, O illustrious dreamer, and bring me back a bunch of daisies from the valley of dreams. No, not daisies, it's the wrong time of year, better make it mushrooms. The edible variety, if that's not too much to ask. See you soon!'

Joseph hung up. With laggard steps, he went over to his desk and sat down. Protected by two thick walls of dictionaries, he filled his fountain pen with black ink. Then he opened a folder bearing the inscription *Treatise on Sleep*. The folder contained several hundred pages but almost all of them were virgin white. As white as the sheets on his bed.

Joseph took a blank page and sat gazing at it. 'Writing, sleeping,' he thought, 'they're very much alike. You stop moving forward and, instead, you go down, deeper and deeper, you open a parenthesis in fate. You are no longer subject to time, you reinvent it. You enter a parallel universe, a different dimension in which all things are possible . . . That's a good thought, I should make a note of it . . .'

With his eyes fixed on the ceiling, Joseph tapped the end of his nose with his pen. He yawned, scratched his head, finally pulled one of the few pages with writing on it out of the folder and read:

> *Is the disturbing increase in the manufacture and*
> *consumption of sleeping pills leading us towards a*
> *massive use of chemicals, aimed at adapting*

*individuals to an environment that becomes ever more
inhuman, to a way of life that is ever more artificial,
and to activities that run more and more counter to
nature? Will there come a day when we are no longer
able to bear other people, nor even ourselves, without
the aid of chemicals?*

*The gross error committed in the case of the
treatment of insomnia has been to consider it as a
disease, whereas it is only symptom, an alarm signal
to warn us that the train is in danger of derailment.*

*Dreams and nightmares permit us to settle our
accounts with the world, they counterbalance our
waking lives, but insomnia tells us: 'You are not
worthy of sleep! You spend your time repressing your
real self, doing things you detest, manipulating
yourself, forcing yourself to keep your mouth shut.
You make decisions with your head instead of
listening to your heart, and yet you still want to sleep!
But sleep doesn't want you! Sleep has to be deserved!
It is a sanctuary, not to be entered with muddy boots
or a snotty nose! If you claim the right to sleep, you
must first open your eyes and learn to cherish your
soul!'*

Joseph crossed out 'soul' and searched for a word to replace it.
He considered for a long time, then he scored out the whole
sentence. A moment later, he sacrificed the paragraph and, on a
sudden impulse – *basta*! – he threw the page into the wastepaper-
basket.

He picked up another sheet covered with notes. He yawned
once more. His eyes were stinging . . . stinging . . . stinging
. . .

. . . they sting, they wing, they zing . . . the page is full of
nasty things that itch and twitch and creep and crawl, and
infiltrate, and irritate, and imitate the words you scrawl . . .
Eeny, meeny, miney, moth . . . moth, moth, chewing cloth . . .
inside the inkpot, beware of jaws . . . paws off, paws off, it's full
of flies with squinty eyes, it's full of bugs with flapping lugs . . .

the table's riddled with squirmy worms, the blotting-paper's mined . . . hands off, fingers off . . . or else . . . or else –
KAPOW!

Joseph woke up with a start, his heart thumping . . . He shook himself, lit a cigarette and made up his mind to settle down seriously to work.

At that moment, Livingstone, exhausted after his ferocious battle with the dead leaf, jumped onto the desk and stretched out lasciviously all over Joseph's papers. Joseph cautiously attempted to part the cat's fur so that he could make a note, but a few indignant swishes of the tail, which sent pens and papers flying, swiftly brought him back to his senses.

He got up, opened the window on the courtyard and once again surveyed his dreamery.

'What an idiot a man must be,' he mused, 'to knock his brains out trying to write a thesis on sleep, which is destined to moulder in the depths of some dusty library, when there are so many, many things he could be dreaming about.'

Gritting his teeth, he looked at his bed with a cold and determined eye. 'I must go in deeper! Move on to serious matters. Sleep, sleep, sleep – all the rest is just waffle! I absolutely *must*, finally, bring something back from down there!'

For a long time now Joseph had been convinced that the assiduous, intensive and methodical practice of sleep, in an experimental frame of mind, could open up limitless vistas to science. Was it not an established fact that numerous discoveries, in a great many fields, had been born during sleep, and that many great artists had found the source of their creativity there? There was really nothing extraordinary about it, since sleep has the virtue of abolishing prejudices of all kinds and removing those psychological blocks that prevent our seeing reality clearly. Sleep wipes out our fear of the truth, the fear which, even more than stupidity, keeps men vegetating in ignorance. Unfortunately, the ordinary sleeper is incapable of drawing any scientific profit from his sleep. In his dreams, the fruits of knowledge brush against his head, but he does not take the trouble to harvest them. He is like a mole who, burrowing through the soil to find a root to gnaw, passes buried treasure without so much as a sidelong glance. For it is fear and desire that lead the dreamer on, not the will to knowledge. But who knows whether a resolute dreamer, one who is ready for anything, perfectly trained and fully aware of the pitfalls of sleep, could not bring back fabulous jewels from his nocturnal explorations? Who knows if the philosophers' stone is not hidden in the depths of sleep? Who knows if dream is not the veritable primary matter of the universe? Who knows if our reality, with its mountains and its rivers, its cities and its deserts, its planets, its suns, its galaxies and its constellations of galaxies, is not simply a particle of dust in the forest of dreams?

Faced with this unknown continent, Joseph was a lone explorer. Nobody had ever encouraged him to sleep. The scientific community looked at him askance, then turned its back on him, regarding him as a mild eccentric, a harmless crank. He could still picture the look on the Director's face when he went to the Foundation that funded scientific research to ask for a grant which would enable him to devote himself exclusively to the practice of sleep. The only way to attract the scientists' attention to his researches would be to come up with some dazzling results. But he had to admit that, up to the present, his explorations had proved fruitless. True, he had made excellent progress in sleeping, he was now a highly experienced sleeper, but something undefined held him back on the threshold of the unknown. It was as if there existed forbidden places in the profoundest layers of sleep, certain doors that must not be opened, certain fatal staircases, certain corridors from which there was no return. Perhaps he was afraid of going too far, of discovering things man was never meant to know. Robert Desnos, a sleeper of genius, had got nothing out of his fanatical practice of sleep except the foreknowledge that he would be sent to Buchenwald.

12

The fate of the great masters of sleep bore testimony that one does not venture into the depths of the land of dreams with impunity. Hölderlin had to be shut up in a tower. Gerard de Nerval hanged himself from some railings one winter's evening. Lovecraft died amidst appalling suffering, imploring the Powers of the night to forgive him. Tartakovitch threw himself out of the window in the asylum where they had confined him . . .

Yes, sleep had claimed its martyrs.

Joseph lit another cigarette and stood looking out of the window. The rain was falling gently, tinkling into the gutters. The elastic step of a cat pattered over the the roof-slates. Joseph looked at the window facing him, on the other side of the courtyard. By the faint light of a moonbeam he could just make out the outline of a piece of furniture. During all the fifteen years he had lived here, he had never once seen a living soul in the house opposite. Perhaps no one had entered it for thirty or forty years. Time seemed to be preserved there, as if at the bottom of a sarcophagus.

The thunderous passing of a dustcart rattled the windows, without, however, waking the cat. Stretched out at full length on the desk, Livingstone was sleeping like a log. 'If he stops me working,' Joseph ruminated, 'he must have his own good reasons for it. Anyway, I have at least made some progress: I've scrapped one page.'

The telephone rang. Sighing, Joseph picked up the receiver.

'Hallo, doctor.' It was the thin, bleating voice of an old lady. 'Listen, I haven't slept a wink . . . I've tried everything . . . I don't know what's the matter with me, I just can't get to sleep . . .'

'Nor can I, Madame, I'm not asleep, either. But it's nothing serious, these things happen sometimes, especially on nights of the full moon.'

'Oh, but I always sleep very well, doctor, even when the moon's full! I've never had insomnia, not even when my husband died . . . do please come, I just know there's something wrong with me . . . and I live just round the corner . . .'

'Well . . .'

2

In the wet, cobbled streets, deliverymen with their arms full of crates were cheerfully exchanging insults, outdoing one another with their witty obscenities. At the windows, cats were poking their noses out between the plants and housewives were viciously beating their pillows. On the pavement, wary and asthmatic pensioners, muffled up in scarves, were walking their poodles. Tradesmen were opening their shops and gossiping with the postman. Teenage secretaries, late for work, were dashing out of front doorways with a great clacking of high heels.

Joseph went into the *Bar des Amis du Sport* and stationed himself at the counter, yawning prodigiously.

The photographs pinned to the walls, under the row of bottles, proclaimed loudly that, in his youth, the *patron* had been captain of the amateur Red Star team. Fat and moustachioed, with glittering eyes and a red nose, he was a dead ringer for Stalin. His regular customers had therefore nicknamed him 'The Father of the People'.

'What can I get you?' he asked Joseph.

'A small coffee with a dash of cognac, please.'

'Coming up.'

'From now on,' Joseph decided, 'house-calls are out, once and for all. I swear it – Cross my heart and swear to die, If I ever tell a lie! – because this is no way to live. As for doling out sleeping pills, not on your life! I don't want to become an accomplice to the chemification of the citizens. And advising them to count sheep is no solution, either . . . What we need is something completely new . . .'

14

Joseph sighed, rubbed his hands over his face and closed his eyes. When he opened them again he saw, in the mirror, a young woman sitting at a table with a *café crème* in front of her.

She had short dark hair and there was something indefinably oriental in her face, with was tinged with melancholy.

Aroused, Joseph searched for some defect in her, so that he could lose interest, but he was unable to find any. Perhaps a line or two around the eyes? No, that only added a little sadness to her beauty. 'Beauty always has a touch of sadness to it,' he said to himself. 'At least, as long as it isn't the kind of sadness that . . .'

'Watch the debate on telly last night, did you?' the *patron* asked him point-blank.

'Er . . . no.'

'Didn't miss much. What a pair of stuffed shirts! Me, I'd send all those glib buggers down the mines . . . make them spend a bit of time down there, all amongst the coal-dust, see what things are really like, from close to . . .'

Joseph nodded agreeement, without taking his eyes off the young woman in the mirror. He had the feeling that he alone could appreciate how beautiful she was. Hers was not the obvious kind of beauty, yet she was fascinating, like a sphinx. A sphinx stirring her *café crème*.

But she was too heavily made-up, and the jewellery she was wearing was in bad taste. She was certainly vulgar. Besides, to come into a bistro like this . . .

'These political whizz-kids,' the *patron* went on, 'they never agree with each other but they all say the same things. If you ask me, they're all in cahoots, for all their squabbling. They're always on about the shabby tricks the other party's up to, but they all sit down and stuff their guts at the same table. Here, here's your coffee with a good dash of cognac . . . You know something? It takes brains to go on talking all the time without ever saying anything! You think it's easy? Not a bit of it, it's hard work being such a prat!'

'Perhaps she's a call-girl who's just finished a night's work,'

15

Joseph thought dejectedly. But then he reassured himself: 'No, not in this district.' Another suspicion crossed his mind: 'Perhaps she's a middle-class housewife, her husband's away and she's just spent the night with her lover . . . Maybe he's a trendy journalist, one of those charming smoothies, a selfish and pretentious smart-arse, the kind all the girls fall for . . . Only he cares as much about her as he does about widows and orphans, that's why she's sad . . .'

'Now,' continued the *patron*, 'if they asked me to run the country . . . Mind you, I wouldn't want the job, but, just for the sake of argument, let's say I was forced to take power, for the good of the country . . . know what I'd do? First, I'd take care of the young 'uns. Send them all out to work in the fields, study nature . . . Then the soldiers, I'd send them off to help the poor in the Third World . . . The old blokes I'd enlist in the army, so they wouldn't be lonely, and, after all, when there isn't a war on, the army's bleeding useless anyway, so it might as well be the old men . . .'

She was slowly sipping her *café crème*, her eyes gazing vacantly ahead of her. Joseph thought fiercely: 'If she's sad, it's quite simply because she still hasn't managed to find the right shoes to go with her new outfit . . . Or she's thinking she'd better shave her legs, something like that . . .'

'Reinstate free public urinals,' the *patron* went on relentlessly, 'because it's degrading having to pay for a pee . . . I'd make hurrying a criminal offence because hurrying sours the blood. No more cars in the cities. Road hogs, straight down the mines. Ban the telly. Local street parties every night, so's people'd get to know each other. Let animals run loose in the streets – ostriches, elephants – because people behave better with animals around. Reduce the workload of the blokes who've got too much and give some to those who haven't got any. Minimum wage for everybody, subject to their learning to play a musical instrument. Reintroduce barter. Compulsory afternoon naps. A garden for everybody. Abolish hunting. Public debates with

16

everyone having their say. At school, scrub mathematics and teach them floriculture. Start cleaning up the Seine . . .'

'Even if it worked out,' said Joseph to himself, 'what good would it do me, to have a woman? A little pleasure, a load of trouble. When you get involved with someone, you start getting jealous, nervous . . . I'd have to listen to her moaning about her shopping, her problems with clothes, her headaches, her moods . . . *basta*! And, if I took a woman home, God knows how Livingstone would react. He's so sensitive he might start wrecking the place. And besides, she'd never understand my work and what it's all about, she'd imagine I sleep for pleasure. No, a woman could only be a hindrance to my researches. Especially just at this moment, when I'm on the point of a breakthrough . . . I can feel it . . .'

'Obviously,' the *patron* conceded, 'the number one priority would be the fight against hunger. But I've got a bright idea about that . . . an idea whose time will come eventually. I talk to all my customers about it and some day the proper authorities will get to hear about it . . .'

Joseph lifted an uncomprehending eye towards his inter-locutor. It was enough to unleash the torrent. With a drying-up cloth in one hand and a wine-glass in the other, his moustache foaming and an exalted look in his eye, The Father of the People barked:

'A pig for everyone! You get me? Pigs can swallow anything, live on all the things we don't eat ourselves. They could be fattened up on our refuse, wouldn't cost a penny and every year we could send the Third World as many pigs as the population of France. Oh, yes, it's dead simple, but it's had to be worked out . . .'

She had finished her coffee and was gazing into the bottom of her cup. Joseph could not help imagining her as an Assyrian princess, caressing a tiger . . . or rather, as an Egyptian slave wearing an anklet . . .

The *patron* was getting more and more heated: 'Main problem

17

is, there are too many of us! Numbers, that's the killer! Ought to send people back to the country, they aren't meant to live in crowds. Man is a beast of the fields. We're advanced monkeys, that's all. Or perhaps, degenerate monkeys . . .'

She was touching up her lipstick. 'I could have a go,' thought Joseph, 'what's the risk? After all, I stand a fair chance, it's not as if I was just anybody.'

He looked in the mirror and saw an anxious face marked by feverish speculations and long-distance voyages through the realms of sleep. What a face, like a disinterred corpse! And he hadn't even shaved! He looked like a maniac just let out of prison. 'It's not possible,' he said to himself, 'the mirror must be warped!'

The *patron*, taking advantage of Joseph's fatigue, was already beginning to expound to him, confidentially, his theory on climate, when the young woman suddenly stood up and left.

Vexed, Joseph consoled himself by crunching a cube of sugar. He remembered the words of Descartes: 'Madame, I love you, but I love the truth still better. Farewell!'

Two minutes later, he was trotting along the road on the heels of the young woman. He had told himself that, if he made no attempt to speak to her, he would be kicking himself for three months. She would certainly send him packing without ceremony, but at least he would be able to go to sleep with a clear conscience.

With his medical bag in his hand, he looked like a schoolboy setting out on his first amorous adventure.

She was wearing a black suit and patent-leather shoes. Her walk, slow, supple and self-assured, had something about it of both the goddess and the animal.

Straightening his tie, Joseph quickened his pace to catch up with her. He watched her serene hips swinging with a cosmic regularity, while his own heart beat like a drum. He thought: 'If I start thinking about what to say, I'll make a mess of it.'

18

A hop, a skip, and there he was beside her.

'Um . . . excuse me, mademoiselle . . .'

She turned towards him with a weary look. Astonished at his own audacity, which he put down to his tiredness, he went on, 'I don't want to seem rude, accosting you like this in the street, I know it's not the done thing, but, er . . . First, let me introduce myself, I'm Dr Joseph Cavalcanti.'

'I'm sorry,' she said, 'but I'm not ill.'

'Ah! But that's not what I had in mind, not at all! I . . . um . . . we were in the same bar . . . the *Amis du Sport*. I saw you in the mirror and . . . how shall I put it? . . . I suddenly felt a desire to know you. You must think me a complete idiot!'

'I've met worse.'

'Well, there it is . . . I couldn't help watching you while I was drinking my coffee and I was wondering why you looked so sad . . .'

'With all the things you see around you,' she replied, 'you'd have to be pretty sick not to feel sad.'

'Oh, yes, you're right there. The world is not exactly cheerful . . . But sadness doesn't solve anything.'

'Being sad can sometimes do you good. Doesn't that ever happen to you? Anyway, you don't exactly look like a gay dog yourself.'

'Oh! Let's just say that, without letting myself be overwhelmed by jollity, I try not to fall into the pit of despair.'

'You avoid extremes, then . . .'

She stopped at a bus stop.

'Well,' she said, 'this is as far as I'm going. I won't detain you, I know a doctor's time is precious. If I fall ill some day, I promise to call on your services.'

'Listen, I'd like to see you again. We could . . . I don't know, we . . . could go somewhere, have a drink. I assure you I'm not a bore. I can even be witty sometimes . . .'

'Don't *tell* me you're witty, make me laugh!'

Annoyed at his own stupidity, he exclaimed:'Good grief! I'm

19

not a performing monkey! I can't make you laugh to order! Give me a little time to get to know you.'

She looked at him with a faint smile and said, 'When you get excited, you don't look so sinister.'

'Huh? . . . Well, we'll see each other again, is that agreed? Look, what would you like to do? What are you interested in?'

'Dinosaurs.'

'Oh,' he said, taken aback. 'Really?'

She did not deign to reply. The bus arrived.

'Listen,' he said brightly, with a presence of mind that he didn't know he had in him, 'perhaps we could go to the Natural History Museum? They've got lots of prehistoric creatures there. For people who like dinosaurs, it's paradise . . .'

The door of the bus opened.

'Well, would you like to come?' Joseph gabbled hurriedly, 'Tomorrow?'

'We'll see tomorrow!'

She got on to the bus, the door closed with a grinding sound and the bus moved off, leaving Joseph nailed to the pavement, bemused, in a cloud of exhaust fumes.

3

'Do you have any books about dinosaurs?'

The old bookseller regarded Joseph with the resigned and weary air of a man who, in the course of his lifetime, has had to listen to the most ludicrous and tiresome questions from sadistic customers who plague him with their outrageous demands.

'You're out of luck,' he replied cruelly. 'I had one that had been in stock for twenty years, but I sold it yesterday. Come back in ten years or so.'

Joseph continued his stroll along the *quais*. They smelled of the Seine, old books and dead leaves. The turbulent sky was full of fat grey clouds. As usually happened when he went out, Joseph had the feeling that he was under a giant lid rather than out in the open air. The sensation of being truly out-of-doors, on a cosmic level, was something he experienced only in dreams.

In fact, he was quickly bored by all the things he saw around him because he had already seen them in his dreams – but on a larger scale, more beautiful and more real. In comparison with his Cinemascope dreams, life seemed to him like a home movie. A home movie devoid of interest or significance. 'Real life is elsewhere,' wrote Rimbaud. For Joseph, real life was in his bed.

Already the street-lamps were lighting up. He decided to go home. He was still feeling tired after his sleepless night, in spite of a long siesta during which he had dreamed of interminable processions of pigs embarking for Africa to the accompaniment of cheering and showers of confetti. He walked towards the Marais district.

On the way, he thought about the girl. He told himself that, if he fell in love, it would diminish his chances. He would become clumsy and self-conscious. In any case, at close quarters, she was nothing to write home about. Her beauty was of the rather cold, inexpressive kind and he would soon tire of it. And then, her so-called mystery, what nonsense! Mystery, in a woman, is always phoney. The wisest thing would be to give up any attempt to see her again.

At all events, he was determined not to start getting ideas. That always led to disappointment. He would try to take her to see the dinosaurs, and afterwards, he would see.

All the same, he should have asked her Christian name . . .

Thunder rumbled. A few minutes later, the storm burst. Joseph, huddled against the sudden downpour, galloped into a doorway and stood sheltering there.

The door was open. At the end of the inner courtyard he saw a worm-eaten sign on which he could just make out . . . TIQUITIES AND SECOND-HA . . . Beside it, there was a staircase leading down to a basement. Joseph decided he might as well browse round this antique shop while waiting for the storm to pass.

He crossed the courtyard under the pelting rain and went down the steps to a glass-panelled door from which a feeble light emanated. As he pushed it open, a little bell tinkled.

The shop was an unbelievable jumble of heteroclite old objects, a hotch-potch of dusty curios amongst which even a bat would not have been able to find her young. There were broken mechanical toys, battered weapons, stuffed tropical birds, mirrors from another age, fragments of asteroids, African fetishes . . . A tarnished showcase held a collection of teeth, from a peaceful molar that had belonged to Pope Boniface VII to the fearsome fang of a tiger shark from the Caribbean sea. Opposite were the death masks of murderers and sundry degenerate characters, displayed on shelves. Beside these, there were some dressmaker's dummies in costume. One of them represented an old Chinaman in traditional dress, with

22

pince-nez and a goatee beard. The eyes seemed positively alive. Joseph went up close to see what material they were made of.

'A good imitation, don't you think?' said the dummy suddenly.

Joseph started. 'Excuse me,' he stammered, 'I thought you were a . . .'

'Hee, hee, hee!' cackled the old Chinaman, whose eyes were sparkling, 'don't apologise, I indulge in this malicious little trick every time an amiable visitor comes to honour me with his presence. When you have looked at nine wax models, you do not perceive that the tenth is a creature of flesh and blood, with a heart that beats. Thus lives the man of merit, ignored, considered as a puppet among puppets . . . But please, excuse these idle and inconsequential remarks which distract me from my duties. May I make so bold as to ask what you are looking for?'

'Well, er, I . . . let's say, I . . . um . . .'

'You do not know what you are looking for! You are right, that is the best way to find it. Here, we have everything, and even more . . . Certainly, at first glance, it seems that the things offered to your sight are not worth looking at. However, it is amongst the brambles and the weeds that the fabulous golden butterfly prefers to hide herself.'

Joseph was already rummaging in the gloomy depths of the little shop, taking care not to bring anything down on his head.

'Incidentally,' he asked, 'you wouldn't by any chance have anything to do with fossil reptiles, something like a dinosaur, for instance?'

'I dislike having to disappoint you, but I fear not, although my modest little shop is vaster than my miserable memory. The latter has declined over the course of the years, while my useless acquisitions have multiplied to excess. I remember well that I once had a diplodocus, but the unlikelihood of such an enormity induces me to believe it must have happened in a dream. Yes, it is undoubtedly too large a creature to inhabit my reality. Strange . . . dreams make us forget many things, but nothing makes us forget our dreams . . . Excuse me, I am talking nonsense. I will

23

leave you to look around. Here, everything is for sale except the spiders' webs and my worthless self. I will merely permit myself to advise you to take your time, without fear of wasting it. The object you will come to love best will not strike the eye immediately. Above all, do not hesitate to ferret into the bottoms of crates and boxes. Happiness lies in little things, and I am sure you will discover some precious little nothing which will soothe your mind, at present agitated by long reflection and scholarly writing.'

Seeing Joseph's astonishment, the old Chinaman added, 'The pallor of your complexion, your wrinkled brow, your sunken eyes, your white hands stained with ink reveal a sorrowful heart, a soul tormented by doubt, a mind plunged into the false delights and the all-too-real agonies of interior voyaging. Please forgive the impertinent frankness and the extreme arrogance of a laughable old man whose long solitude has caused him to lose all sense of etiquette, but, although I do not know where you are going, allow me to advise you to turn back. Do not be like the chimpanzee who, believing coconuts were no longer good enough for him, sat with his nose in the air, dreaming of eating the moon. Give up all idea of descending into the volcano with your dark-lantern in your hand. There is still time to turn back. Perhaps there are sleeping monsters in the depths of your mind, what good will it do to waken them?'

'But isn't it human nature, wanting to know yourself?' Joseph asked, still rummaging in the dusty cavern.

'If the caterpillar learns that he is a caterpillar, will he become a butterfly? It is through knowledge that men have begun to "rectify" nature, like children who wish to teach their mothers. Like fish who would like to invent something better than water. Why must one always be asking oneself "why"? Knowledge creates a desert around itself.'

'But it raises man towards the light!' Joseph exclaimed ardently, his finger pointing up to a dilapidated chandelier that was clinging to the ceiling by a few bits of string.

'The moth is attracted to the light and burns his wings in the flame.'

'Perhaps it is better to burn than to settle for a cosy life in bedroom slippers . . . Oh! You have records, too?'

From under an African figurine, Joseph pulled a 78 that must have dated from before the Flood.

'That is the only one I possess,' replied the old Chinaman, 'I believe it is a jazz record. Do you like jazz?'

'No, but my cat's mad about it.'

Joseph dusted off the sleeve with the cuff of his raincoat and read: *Black Papa and the Dormouse Band*. The tune was entitled *Sleep Party*.

'Here's something that interests me,' he said.

The old Chinaman hesitated imperceptibly then said, 'It's probably scratched . . .'

'It doesn't matter.'

'. . . and certainly warped.'

'Never mind, I'll take it.'

'Good,' sighed the old man, 'that will be five francs.'

Joseph paid. 'For the moment,' he said, 'I'll say goodbye, and thanks for your wise counsel!'

'It is I who must thank you for your delightful visit,' replied the old Chinese, bowing, 'as well as for your indulgence in listening to the tiresome digressions of an insignificant and doddering old man.'

The rain had let up a little.

Joseph had some shopping to do but decided to put it off till next day. After all, he still had some spaghetti and a tomato or two.

Hurrying home, he reflected on the words of the old Chinaman. 'Perhaps he's right, perhaps knowledge is a fall from grace. Certainly, the man who understood everything would go mad. Ah, I should never have started thinking! *Basta*! It's too late now, I can't jump off the moving train. I must go on to the end, hold on a bit longer. I feel I'm just about to land a really big fish . . . Pfoof! I've been telling myself that for ten years. . . Ah, well, at least I've never prostituted my conscience. I can live at peace with myself, and that's worth more than gold. There are people who bust a gut to climb the greasy pole and snatch the prize from the top, but, for myself, I prefer to go down into the depths of unexplored abysses . . . even if I find nothing there but dead rats. In the end, the most important thing is not to know where you're heading, otherwise it would all become so boring and exhausting. No, really to spend one's life sitting in a well-oiled chromium-plated office chair, doing nothing that hasn't been done a thousand times before, having nothing in your head but "received ideas", repressing the desire to dream, tramping along the old beaten track of the mind, no, that's not my scene! My way is to risk my skin every night, in bed. Perhaps, one fine morning, I won't be able to find the way back . . . tough luck! If you want to hit the bull's eye, you have to aim high!'

These were the reflections of Joseph Cavalcanti as he walked home through the rain, trying to protect the probably scratched and certainly warped record under his indisputably moth-eaten raincoat. Since the said garment was waterproof in name only, Joseph soon found himself drenched to the skin. Then, in a gesture of exaltation, he lifted his head and offered his face to the rain. At the same moment, he stepped into a puddle and felt the water seep into his shoe from below. There must be a hole in the sole. Instantly deflated, he told himself anxiously that he would have to buy a new pair of shoes. This was the kind of chore that brought him out in a cold sweat, like writing a letter to a government department or finding a willing and sympathetic plumber to mend a leaky tap. The worst of it was that this inability to cope with little things was getting worse by the month, almost by the day. Any activity, other than reading or sleeping, gave him the horrors. Worse! Reading made his eyes ache after ten minutes and sometimes he could not even be bothered to go to bed.

'Perhaps I'm turning into a monster,' he said to himself, examining his hands anxiously. But he thought of the words of Ramakrishna: 'Despise not the man who lies yawning in his hammock while others bend their backs to the plough, for he alone will dare to face the tiger.'

4

The cat stalked round the record, sniffing it from all sides.

'Patience, my dear Livingstone,' said Joseph, 'tomorrow I'll go down to the cellar and get the old record-player.'

Whilst cooking his spaghetti, Joseph again began thinking about the young woman. Tomorrow morning, he would try to see her. He decided to go to bed early so as to be in good shape.

He took a shower and then opened his wardrobe, which had a mirror on its door. Inside hung his one and only suit, with his forty pairs of pyjamas lined up beside it. He reviewed them carefully and finally selected a pair of ceremonial Chinese pyjamas in black silk embroidered with gold. An impeccable costume is essential to the scientific practice of sleep. It fortifies the self-confidence of the dreamer. Besides, one never knows where a dream will lead, so it is best to be presentable at all times.

That night, Joseph was determined to travel far. The boldness he had displayed in accosting the young woman had bolstered his self-confidence. He felt keyed up.

The cat was already sitting on the eiderdown, choosing a spot with meticulous care. After mature consideration, he opted for his usual place, the south-east corner of the bed. Having made a little hollow, he curled himself cosily into a ball with his paws well tucked in and his nose buried in his fur.

Joseph lit a cigarette and went over to the window. As always, he spent a long time looking at the window opposite, on the other side of the courtyard. There was an abandoned apartment there, a segment of the past, enclosed and inaccessible . . . and he who, in dreams, had travelled to countries that do not appear on any map, traversed interminable Siberias, mysterious Indias and unheard-of Chinas, sailed oceans without name and crossed deserts measureless to man while snoring under the blankets, he who, lulled by the ticking of his alarm clock, had explored the subterranean palace of the Queen of Sheba and the Hanging Gardens of Babylon, he, Joseph Cavalcanti, whose oneiric geography would have supplied material for hundreds of atlases, would never enter that room just a few metres away. . .

With a sigh, he stubbed his cigarette out in an ashtray. After disconnecting the telephone, he went over to the bed, checked to make sure there were no monsters lurking under it, resolutely kicked off his slippers and slid between the sheets.

Yawning, he turned his head and looked at the bedside table. Beside the log-book in which he recorded his dreams was a pile of his favourite bedside books: *The Life of Christopher Columbus* by Ernest Pigeon, *The Steps of Sleep* by Rollenstein, *Dreams and How to Direct Them* by the Marquis d'Hervey-Saint-Denys, *Some Phenomena of Sleep* by Charles Nodier, the *Oneirocritic* by Artemidorus, as well as the sleeper's Bible, the *Hypnometron* by the great master of sleep, Amédéor Tartakovitch. Joseph had had to steal a moth-eaten but extremely rare copy of this legendary work from the damp and gloomy basement of a library in Budapest.

These books on sleep in no way possessed the virtue of sending Joseph to sleep – quite the contrary. But he also had to hand a pile of recent novels, every one crowned with literary prizes, whose marvellously soporific powers he greatly appreciated. Was it not admirable that, in a country where insomnia was reaching epidemic proportions, there should be so many writers ardently devoting themselves to the noble task of sending their neighbours to sleep? At least, that is what Joseph said to himself as he tried to decipher one page by an author who was all the rage, hyped by the media, and whose entire art consisted in stringing together little snippets of nonsense with brio and virtuosity. It was of a brilliant nullity, a grandiloquent vacuity, contrived with the sole aim of dazzling the reader. It glittered with intelligence, but the whole thing rang hollow. Each line possessed that vulgar distinction, that eye-catching refinement of the parvenu who drinks his tea with his little finger crooked, that pseudo-aristocracy of the flashy adventurer-of-letters who spreads his culture on like jam and shows off his style like a whore showing off her arse. It was a novel written not for the enjoyment of the reader, but to make him admire the author. The work of a charlatan of the written word, a pseudo-intellectual who strove constantly to pander to the frustrations, the voyeurism and the narcissism of the reader, instead of chucking a good bucketful of cold water into his face to wake him up.

After a few pages, the book fell from Joseph's hands. He had reached the limit of human endurance.

'You know what I call this, Livingstone?' he asked, yawning like a whale.

Without waiting for the cat's reply, he went on, 'It's windbag literature, it puffs itself up with words. Between ourselves, Livingstone, performing one's natural functions with courage and conviction is much less vulgar than spinning fine phrases when one has nothing whatsoever to say.'

By way of comment, the cat raised his head slightly, yawned voluptuously and curled himself once more into a snug ball.

'You're absolutely right,' said Joseph. 'Happy the man who is his own refuge!'

He picked up the alarm clock and wound it carefully. No need to set the alarm, since the cat took it upon himself to wake him every morning on the stroke of seven. Generally, after giving Livingstone his breakfast Joseph went back to bed, but tomorrow he would go to the *Amis du Sport* to see the girl again.

He put the clock back on the night-table and gazed at it for a moment. There was nothing remarkable about it, but therein lay its originality. It was a Soviet alarm-clock dating from the fifties. A perfectly adequate alarm clock, conceived without an ounce of imagination, but with exemplary rigour, by admirable engineers, an austere, sober, strictly funtional machine, a standard mechanism with implacable hands, an inexorable tick-tock and a blood-curling alarm: the very image of Time.

Joseph switched off the bedside lamp. 'Courage!' he said to himself as he pulled the eiderdown over his head.

At this moment, nobody could do him any harm, he no longer had anything to fear, he was snug and warm in his darkness, all alone, well-protected from everything. His bed was an impregnable fortress, an indestructible light-house built on a rock in the midst of a raging sea. Outside, anything might happen, he cared no more about it than about his very first pair of pyjamas. The soft warmth of his sheets was eternal. Even if the earth shattered into a thousand fragments, he would float out into space aboard his flying bed, immortal beneath his eiderdown.

No, he no longer had anything to fear. Except his own thoughts.

He started thinking about his solitude. The solitude he pretended to love, to have chosen, and which had moved in with him, slowly but surely, over the years. His friends had drifted away, shrivelled up inside their petty, dreary existences illumined by the TV, proud of their kids and their cars, satisfied with a life whose sole litany was: *soon it'll be the weekend, soon the holidays, soon retirement*, and dreaming of creating an idyllic island all of their own in the midst of a world that was churning in a sea of dish-water. Perhaps they were right . . . no, they were wrong. To spend your whole life thinking of nothing but your material security is to run the greatest of all risks. Cowardice is more dangerous than courage. In any case, as far as his friends were concerned, it was over. Friendships do not last unless there is a common ambition. When you are young, you dream about the same things together. As time passes, you become aware that it is in the nature of dreams to remain just that: dreams. But Joseph had never renounced his dreams. Result: he had become a monster. A sad monster whose sole passion was sleeping. Yes, a monster . . . and yet no, not even that. A monster is alive, it belches, it farts, it roars, it sweats, it kicks over the traces, rolls on the ground, spitting in all directions . . . None of that was for him. He had remained courteous, urbane, civilised. He did not even gnaw the bars of his cage, nor stick his head out of the window to insult the passer-by. He was like a well-oiled automaton. Well-oiled for suffering. An anxiety pump, that's what he was, a machine designed to worry itself which functioned with the regularity of a clock. From the social point of view, he was dead. Nobody would have risked a bet on him. His researches had been marking time for years. He was making no progress, he was running round and round like a rat in a maze. He was nothing to nobody. His only moments of pleasure in life were when he forgot about life – when he was as drunk as a skunk or sleeping like a log. He felt himself to be an alien to everything, like an extra-terrestrial. It was not as if he had no love to give, he had plenty, but it turned back upon itself. In fact, he loved too much, that was why he had become solitary and unsociable. He would have to watch himself: those who love too much become a public menace. One day, they would come and take him away and lock him up . . . Ah, damn it all! He was having a fit of the blues. (That was what he called these crises of anxiety under the eiderdown.) However, he had sworn never to think about his life when he was immobile. Unless you are physically very tired, immobility breeds distorted ideas and black thoughts.

He turned over on to his other side, envying the cat who was sleeping as if on the wings of angels.

Think of something cheerful. Tahiti, for instance. Ah! The beach, the sun, the coconut palms, the ukuleles . . . And the women, women everywhere, hidden in the bushes like Easter eggs, women on the beach, in the street, cat-women, bird-women, barley-sugar women, chocolate women, women of every colour, women who would love him with their whole hearts simply because they would see him as he really was. He would live by hunting and fishing. He would live amongst animals, gods and children, amongst beings whose sole concern was loving. And she would be there, she . . .

How had she managed to live up till now without his knowing? How had he managed to live without knowing her? What did she do? What did she like? What sort of home did she have? Did she have a lover? How many legs did she have. . . ?

. . . All the things he was visualising began to take on a life of their own, to escape his control, to breed and proliferate ever more rapidly, like some delirious, speeded-up film. His imagination took flight, his brain let rip, racing full speed ahead in a swarm of living ciphers, a firework display of frenzied scribbles and coloured bubbles . . .

It was, at one and the same time, totally incoherent and rigorously logical. The rough draft of reality.

. . . Faster and faster came the darkness. The tick-tock of the alarm clock speeded up, the bed accelerated . . . At the window, giant, brilliantly-lit refineries glided past in the night, followed by whole cemeteries of cars, tower-blocks as smooth as cubes of ice, railway lines with their points inextricably tangled. It was a desert of concrete, asphalt and steel. Amongst the stars twinkled advertisements for super-powerful detergents, natural yoghurt and trips to Tahiti. A luminous ham was dangling from the moon.

Joseph did not recognise this city. 'Damn!' he said to himself, 'I've got on the wrong train again. And, what's more, I haven't got a ticket.' At this moment, the ticket-collector arrived. It was The Father of the People.

'Tickets, please,' he said.

'You've come at just the right moment,' said Joseph, 'I don't happen to have a ticket.'

'No ticket!' exclaimed The Father of the People, rolling his 'r's', even though there are no 'r's' in 'no ticket'.

'Don't worry,' Joseph went on, 'I don't need one. I'm dreaming.'

'Stone the crows, that's no excuse!' yelled The Father of the People indignantly. 'If everybody started dreaming without tickets, we'd be in a fine old mess!'

Joseph rummaged apprehensively in his pockets. And to think, it would have been so easy to get a ticket before going to bed!

The Father of the People, eyebrows scowling and moustache bristling, threatened, 'If you don't give me your ticket at once, I'll make you regret the day you were born!'

Joseph attempted to change the subject. 'What's that?' he asked, pointing to something outside the train.

'Shit cannon,' replied The Father of the People.

And, in fact, between two enormous domes that looked like observatories, a gigantic cannon had been set up. From its mouth, tons of filth were being ejected in a steady stream to become satellites in the cosmos. High, high above, amongst the stars, could be seen plastic bottles, old tyres, tins and the carcasses of wrecked cars, slowly rotating in eternity.

'Good idea, that!' said Joseph. 'Economical, discreet and no more nasty smells!'

The Father of the People scratched the tip of his nose with a crucifix and declared, 'Space on the ground has become so expensive that all the refuse, hey, presto! They just shoot it up into the air.'

'Couldn't they dig a little hole?' asked Joseph, pretending to be interested in the problem.

'Oh! it's already full up down here. There are so many people there's no more room.'

Then he made a grotesque and frightening gesture which meant both 'under' and 'lying down'. It curdled Joseph's blood.

His entrails churning with anguish, he tried to tone down what The Father of the People had said. 'Nothing? Nothing? That's a bit exaggerated, surely. . . ?'

By way of reply, The Father of the People took off his cap, spat into it and put it back on his head. Then he stuck a label over the door of the compartment which read: MUST PAY. And out he went.

34

When the train stopped, Joseph assumed a nonchalant air and did not get out. A moment later, it started again. And it went on and on and on and on . . . (At least, Joseph had the impression, perhaps fleeting, that it went on for a very long time.)

At last, the train came to a halt in a small disused provincial station. Joseph stepped out on to the deserted platform and crossed the empty waiting-room, where tropical plants were growing. Then he left the abandoned station and found himself in the jungle.

It was a vast forest, the tree-tops were hidden in the clouds and the leaves were so enormous that he could have stretched out on them, as if in a hammock. Spiders' webs as big as the sails of a ship were suspended between the trunks. The ground was treacherous. He had to tread very gingerly over rotten tree-stumps covered in moss, holding on to trailing lianas so as not to fall into a hole. Joseph picked his way slowly through this vegetable chaos, making every effort to pass unnoticed.

Unnoticed by whom or what, he did not know. Still less did he want to know.

Suddenly he saw a human skeleton curled up on the ground among some giant lettuces. Probably the remains of a dreamer who had lost his way. Some tall spotted flowers were swaying in a deathly silence. The Worst was lying in wait everywhere. Joseph walked on as if he was not afraid and, so as not to attract the horror, composed his features into the expression of a man who is comfortably at home. He was also careful not to stare at things, so as not to give them time to metamorphose themselves.

He began to hum, although there was a risk that this would give away his presence. But, whatever the cost, he had to stifle his more and more intrusive imagination.

With his throat tied in knots, he hummed:

> *'I've got a gherkin*
> *Here in my jerkin . . .'*

Unfortunately, the words themselves were invested with something unspeakable that undermined their sense, and the word *gherkin* suddenly seemed to him the very pit of abomination.

At the very moment when the Worst seemed certain to happen, Joseph arrived at a bandstand.

It stood at the edge of a high cliff overlooking a grandiose valley.

Inside, the old Chinese antique dealer was sitting on a swing and each forward movement carried him out over the void.

'Phew!' said Joseph, 'I got through alive, but only by the skin of my teeth. Anyway, a little sport does you good!'

'Especially when you're asleep,' replied the old Chinaman.

Joseph looked up at the limpid sky and went on, 'And it doesn't alter the fact that the weather's glorious. It's hard to believe I'm tucked up under my eiderdown.'

Then he climbed up into the bandstand and approached the edge of the cliff. The sky was of an antediluvian blue, a blue so profound and so pure that one could see the constellations shining. The valley stretched away as far as the eye could see, with endless prairies and titanic trees. Down there, very far off, at a distance of several days' walk and several nights' dreaming, a river sparkled serenely.

'I don't see any philosophers,' said Joseph, astonished. (He had meant to say 'dinosaurs'.)

The old Chinaman scratched his ear and a rainbow appeared. At the end of the valley, some living creatures began to move. They were dinosaurs.

'Are they tame?' asked Joseph.

'It depends how you treat them,' replied the old Chinaman. 'They have their little moods, like everybody else.'

'Why have they vanished from the earth?'

'Go and ask them,' said the old Chinese.

And, still sitting on his swing, he intoned a sad lullaby.

Watching the dinosaurs browsing in this blessed valley, Joseph was smitten with nostalgia. 'One day,' he said to himself, 'I shall be like them.'

Ah! If only he could bring one back from his sleep, what a triumph it would be! Of course, a dinosaur is rather heavy to transport, it takes up a lot of room in a bed, but, afterwards, his problems would be over! He would receive the Nobel Prize for Sleep and eat *marrons glacés* every day.

In the bandstand, there were some fluffy little toy dinosaurs. Joseph waited until the old man was looking the other way, then nicked one and slipped it discreetly into his underpants. But the dinosaur made an embarrassing lump in his trousers. It would be wiser to make himself scarce.

'I'm going to take advantage of the fact that I'm asleep to do a little shopping,' he said, 'see you later!'

The old Chinaman, pointing to a staircase that led down from the floor of the bandstand, replied:

'Later is always downwards. Go straight down, you can't miss it.'

Several dreams later, or possibly later on in the same dream, Joseph, after walking for ages through deserted underground passages, found himself in a supermarket.

The place was crowded with consumers who were as unaware of each other as damned souls in hell. From force of habit, Joseph made for the bookshelves. There, he could not believe his eyes: there were edible books, throw-away books, tinned books, bio-degradable books, books whose pages had to be turned with a handle, talking books, books made of plush, like Teddy Bears, plastic books, books with a mini-TV built in, and write-it-yourself books.

Joseph did not linger because, just beside a shelf of multi-religious cults, there was an erotic shelf that immediately excited his curiosity. There were miniature women swimming in tiny aquariums, and mechanical male love-apparatuses as well as female ones that resembled slot-machines.

Joseph felt suffocated. He went towards the exit but, the nearer he got to it, the more the crowd pressed about him. The consumers were swarming round the central check-out, begging to be given priority, showing their brim-full trolleys as proof of their goodwill.

Some of them began to sing in a servile fashion, moving their trolleys in time to the music. Others, who had fallen and were being trampled on by the rhythmically swaying mass, sang even louder to demonstrate their zeal and in the hope of being allowed to get up. Thinking it best not to make himself conspicuous, Joseph joined in the chorus:

> Oh, I'm a really good consumer,
> I shop in the best of humour
> And buy all the goodies I can
> To make myself a better man.
> I rush from store to store
> Buying more and more:
> Yoghurt to save me getting madder,
> Mineral water for my bladder,
> Oh, I'm a really good consumer,
> I shop in the best of humour . . .

The exit was a station-hall as big as a cathedral. The girl at the check-out officiated solemnly from behind an altar. Joseph was afraid she would not let him pass. Not only had he bought nothing but, worse, he did not have any money to pay with. He therefore started making eyes at the girl, who turned out to be the young woman from the *Amis du Sport*.

He had only to give her a few telling looks and she was seduced.

Joseph, being an opportunistic dreamer, ever ready to seize on a stroke of good luck, pushed his way through the crowd, climbed up on to the altar and lay down on his back. The check-out girl, with her eyes glittering and her tongue hanging out, climbed on to the altar after him and, panting with excitement, hoisted up her skirt.

Meanwhile, the consumers who were queueing up at the altar began to protest: 'It's disgusting! Doing that here, in front of everybody! And him a doctor, too! He ought to be ashamed!'

'But, since I'm dreaming,' pleaded Joseph, 'I have every right to . . .'

'You! Well, sir, *you* may be dreaming, but we're not!'

The check-out girl began to make a fuss, hesitating to sit on top of him and declaring that, under normal circumstances, he should have produced a certificate of authenticity.

'Hurry up and do it!' he said, 'I've got a train to catch! I have to wake up at seven o'clock!'

At that moment he saw, under the altar, a giant alarm clock swinging slowly on the end of a cable. The hands indicated seven o'clock.

'Don't worry,' said the check-out girl, 'it's not an alarm clock, it's a sleep-machine. There's no danger of your waking up.'

The consumers were getting vicious. They called Joseph a savage and a filthy pervert and tried to bite him. He took hold of the check-out girl by the armpits and sat her down on top of him. As she started moving up and down astride his belly, he lashed out with his feet in an effort to repel the crowd of customers, who were determined to gnaw his legs.

The girl was getting heavier and heavier. Suddenly she started shouting, 'Lousy dreamer! Oh, why do I always end up with dreamers? Crazy poets baying at the moon!'

At the same time, she was crawling up his body and he saw that she was pregnant right up to the chin. Pregnant with a dinosaur.

Finally, she sat on Joseph's chest and squeezed his head between her moist thighs. By this time, she weighed several tons. Joseph was suffocating. Suddenly she picked up a rubber stamp which was lying on the altar and began bashing him in the face with it, yelling, 'That's for Mum! That's for Dad! That's for Gran! And that's for Auntie Vera!'

Joseph let out a howl – and woke up.

The cat was lying on his head, calmly sharpening his claws on the pillow. Joseph heaved him off.

His body was bathed in sweat, his heart pounding like a steam-hammer. 'This time,' he said to himself, 'I heard the bullet whistling past my ear. I really thought I'd had it.' He invariably felt this morbid sensation of having been within a hair's breadth of never waking up again.

As happened every morning at seven sharp, Livingstone, after honing his claws on the pillow, granted Joseph thirty seconds grace to get up. Since he was still in bed when this brief truce had expired, the cat let out a single 'Miaouw', free of charge, as a final ultimatum and then serenely attacked the wallpaper. Cold-bloodedly, scrupulously, he set about tearing it to shreds with tooth and claw.

Joseph brought one hand out from under the eiderdown, groped around on the floor, seized a slipper and threw it at the cat. Livingstone, accustomed to this last-ditch strategy, easily dodged the missile and conscientiously set to work again, ripping the wallpaper in a precise and methodical manner.

'Tyrannical bloody cat!' shouted Joseph, but he finally got up and, stupefied with sleep, tottered towards the kitchen, one foot slippered, the other bare.

Livingstone immediately abandoned his destructive tactics and shot across to the fridge like a rocket.

5

'Do you think they used to let people stroke them?' she asked, her eyes raised to the skeleton of a tyrannosaurus.

Since the morning, Joseph had been living as if in a beautiful dream. He had found the young woman at the bus stop again and, miraculously, she had immediately accepted his invitation to the Museum. Having made a date to meet there later, he spent the morning in a state of euphoria. Hope lent him wings: in the space of a few hours, he had accomplished more than in a whole year of mere existence. Watched anxiously by the cat, he had vacuumed the whole flat, changed the sheets (you never know your luck), dusted his books and cleaned the kitchen. Then he had gone out again, bought a pair of shoes, a new umbrella, a tie the colour of a dinosaur and a *Teach Yourself* book about fossil saurians, which he had read at the barber's.

Although chronically unpunctual, he had arrived on time for the appointment at the Museum and – Miracle No. 2! – she was already there, dressed in a mouse-grey suit and standing in front of the skeleton of a giant carnivore. She was not wearing make-up. He found her even more beautiful than the first time.

While she was contemplating the tyrannosaurus, he contemplated her, enraptured.

'Are you on Cloud Nine or something?' she said, turning towards him.

'Eh? . . . Oh, did they let themselves be stroked? . . . The fact is, the problem never arose. Man did not appear until seventy million years after they'd become extinct. But, in my

41

opinion, those beasts wouldn't have been very sensitive to gestures of affection.'

He lifted his eyes to the nightmarish fossil that reared up before him and added, 'If this specimen was alive, I think he'd hardly have given us time to introduce ourselves. For thousands of centuries, this creature was lord of the earth, the most terrible carnivore of all time, the *Tyrannosaurus rex*. Twenty tons of armour-plated flesh, jaws fit to crunch up an elephant, claws like sabres, eyes that could penetrate the darkest night, muscles that could uproot a baobab tree . . . and a brain no bigger than a peanut. His obsession was eating. His one and only idea was to kill. Perhaps he knew nothing of fear, since there was nothing that could frighten him. He didn't need to think, he was the mightiest of them all. He caught everything he saw, devoured everything that moved. He was an eating machine.'

'Why did God make such a monster?' she asked dreamily.

'Perhaps, at that time, God himself was still a child . . . But, anyway, the tyrannosaurus is only a monster when seen from the viewpoint of *Homo sapiens*, a pretentious animal with a hyper-trophied brain. Who knows whether, when it comes right down to it, God didn't take more pride in this creature than in any other? When the extra-terrestrial palaeontologists come to study the history of life on our planet (by which time it will be nothing but a grey desert blanketed in a noxious fog), they will no doubt regard the *Tyrannosaurus rex* as the jewel of Creation, the King of Life, for he reigned much longer than we poor humans will – we were no sooner born than threatened with extinction. And yet, in spite of his all-powerfulness, nature did away with him. She swept him clean off the face of the earth, like a straw. He had had his hour, now he is forever nothing.'

'I wonder how they managed to make babies,' she said.

'Oh, nothing could be simpler! The gentleman dinosaur put his thing into the lady dinosaur's thing and, hey presto! In spite of science and technological progress, nobody's found a better way yet.'

'Shall we go and see the diplodocus?'

Her name was Sonia and she worked at the *Styx*, a nightclub in the Marais, where she did 'an artistic number'. She lived alone.

Suddenly, it struck Joseph that he could go crazy for this woman. He had charged, head down, into a hellish trap.

The feeling that had always dominated his existence was a sort of painful serenity, a calm sorrow interspersed with crises of exaltation and fits of depression. He lived in melancholy the way a fish lives in water. It enveloped him, protected him, kept him warm, like his books. Wasn't there a danger that love would upset this tranquil and dreamy bitterness in which he was so snugly muffled? A risk that his daily routine as a hardened bachelor would become unbearable and he would take a dislike to all his sacred little habits?

He tried to fight against it. He considered the girl with the implacable eye of a dinosaur. He said to himself, 'What use is a woman, if you can't eat her?'

Then, while she was leaning over some fossil collections, he examined her from a strictly palaeontological point of view. 'Female specimen of hominid of the species *Homo sapiens*,' he thought, 'she's beautiful, but no more so than a dinothere's tusk.'

The museum was deserted. The rain reverberated on the glass roof, the parquet flooring creaked beneath their feet. From time to time they saw a warden's cap perched on the skull of a megalosaurus.

With the tips of her red-varnished nails she stroked the horn of a triceratops.

'That would hurt,' she said.

They sat down on a bench in front of the carcase of a brontosaurus. Joseph felt fine. He was savouring the quietness and the placid warmth of this woman close beside him. He would have liked to close his eyes and fall asleep leaning against her. She had a serene femininity, a self-assurance that was tranquil and soothing, a feline womanliness that seemed to have all the time in the world – that seemed, indeed, to dispose of Time. Her way of being, her sensual rhythm, her panther-like tempo, was in total contrast to all the frenzy of modern life. She had nothing in common with those frantic, chattering females who imagine themselves to be free because they are completely dominated by the masculine dynamic and pride themselves on knowing, like men, how to chase the carrot-on-a-stick. In no way did she resemble those stress-bedevilled people who fight a perpetual battle against time, and live against the grain in the delusion that they are doing more, acquiring more, and living more fully whereas, in reality, they are simply being gobbled up by time. With her silence, her immobility, her slow gaze, she set everything around her in order and made any kind of agitation seem ridiculous. She dwelt amongst humans like a pearl in an ant-hill.

In her presence, Joseph did not feel obliged to talk. In the company of any woman whatsoever, the fundamental rule, the inviolable law had always seemed to be: *Keep your lips moving at all costs. Silence prohibited*. And he had always considered it more dignified and more humane to practise continence rather than force himself to chatter to a woman for hours on end, and be constrained to listen to her for days, with the sole aim of seducing her. But with this girl, it was quite different; silence was not taboo. When she spoke, it was not to fill up a void but because she had something to say. It was not to kill silence but to give it some savour.

Nevertheless, he was afraid she might be bored. Swinging his umbrella between his legs, he said, 'So you like all these fossils, do you?'

'Yes' she replied. 'They make a change from everyday monsters. And besides, skeletons are restful. Perhaps because they make one think of all the time that has passed, all those millions of years . . . And those other millions that will pass when we are gone . . . Just think, one day we will be nothing . . . that's really something, isn't it?'

44

'Pshaw!' said Joseph. 'Perhaps our nothingness will be richer than our lives. When we have become nothing, well . . . we will be everything. We shall sleep in peace in the warm bosom of the earth. And when the world blows up, we will be transformed into a dream, into motes of dust . . .'

And, with his umbrella, he traced a majestic curve above the brontosaurus.

She laughed mockingly, 'We shall be nothing but a few little shrivelled-up atoms, lost in some corner of an enormous galaxy.'

'It is only within our minds that things are large or small,' he replied, 'but in terms of the cosmos, these notions make no sense. The tiniest grain of dust counts just as much as a thousand billion suns. As for nothingness, it's meaningless. It exists only inside our limited brains. Nothingness – you could spend all eternity talking about it without arriving at any real conception of it.'

'Meanwhile, I have a little bit of nothingness inside me. Could we go and eat a cake or something?'

'Certainly,' he replied (but not with a very good grace because now he was launched upon sublime things and in the mood to continue).

Out in the street, he thought: 'She has no imagination. But after all, since nothingness is totally unimaginable, her lack of imagination may bring her nearer to the truth than I am . . .'

'Look out!' she cried, jerking him back by the arm. 'You almost got yourself run over!'

'There is something . . . I don't know what it is, something tragic in your eyes,' he said, pouring out the tea.

She cut off a piece of her rum baba with a knife and said, before putting it into her mouth, 'You, too. You have a sorrowful air, like a night-cap.'

'It's your beauty that makes me sad . . .' he answered, biting mournfully into his cream cake.

45

'Sorry. You can always look at something else.'

'. . . and besides, I am reminding myself that, in a little while, I won't be with you any longer.'

'Oh, so being with me makes you sad because you're thinking that you're going to be sad at *not* being with me any more. If you don't mind my saying so, I think you're tying yourself up in knots. You're in danger of tripping yourself up.'

'It's my nature to question myself. I really enjoy overcoming problems, rising above dreary realities . . .'

'In that case, you're in danger of banging your head on the ceiling.'

'Shometimesh that happensh,' he said, solemnly munching his cream cake.

The tea-rooms were full but, as the customers were distinguished people, there was little noise. Some old, world-weary members of parliament, dead from the neck up, were choosing cakes from menus that trembled in their palsied hands; a number of stout old dowagers, smothered in pearls, were prattling to each other as they tore at their strawberry tarts; some devotees of the Stock Exchange, having spread out their newspapers behind their *gâteau Saint-Honoré*, were calculating their profits, while a scattering of gigolos, raising their cups daintily to their lips, eyed the tottery old ladies of private means who, weighed down by their fat and their jewels, were looking for a vacant table.

'It's delightful here,' said Joseph, in an attempt to dispel the unspeakable atmosphere of the place.

He took a stealthy glance at himself in a mirror. With his teacup in his hand, his freshly barbered hair and chin and his new tie, he thought he looked rather aristocratic. To be precise, like a Spanish grandee. An *aficionado* of bulls and roses. An austere dignity radiated from him. The authority of the scientist mingled with the intuitive assurance of the poet. He raised his chin a little and put on a mildly disdainful expression. With a monocle, he would have been perfect.

'Do you look after mad people?' Sonia asked abruptly.

Joseph started and his imaginary monocle fell out. 'Beg pardon?'

'Well, you told me you were a doctor, so I thought perhaps you worked with nutters . . . you seem to me to have a slightly . . . um . . . original air.'

'No, I'm not a psychiatrist, although I often have to deal with patients who are, shall we say, slightly cracked. So I do see nutters, as you call them, but my speciality is disorders of sleep.'

'Oh really? Then you can help me. I have these dinosaurs that stop me sleeping. That's why I'm interested in the creatures. Every time, just as I'm about to drop off, bingo! there's a dinosaur showing me his teeth. It's as if he were guarding the gates of sleep. So I have to take sleeping pills.'

'You mustn't. Sleeping pills induce a false sleep, they intoxicate and upset the whole organism.'

'But what can I do? Count sheep?'

'No, tame the dinosaurs. In other words, think about your insomnia. A lot of people believe that going to sleep is turning their backs on reality, or on themselves. In fact, it's exactly the opposite. Sleep is a descent into the lower depths of the self, into the dungeons of consciousness, the dark caverns of your own mind, where you stash away higgledy-piggledy all the things you don't want to know about, everything you fear most . . . and everything you love too much. To sleep is to see your life from the wings. The reverse side of the scenery seems to us absurd and incoherent, but that's because the *trompe l'oeil* effect is no longer deceiving us. Dreams are our lives, but in a truer form. When we close our eyes, we lose our blindness. Our efforts to delude ourselves are interrupted at the same time as our consciousness, and there we are, face to face with ourselves. Our existence blows up, slaps us in the face, our nature avenges itself for what we impose on it, it rebels against the demands we make on it. If you suffer from insomnia, it's because you're afraid to sleep. You're afraid of finding yourself, naked as a worm, before the judgement seat of sleep.'

47

She looked down and contemplated the bottom of her cup. After a moment, she said, 'So there's no cure for dinosaurs?'

'No,' he replied, laughing, 'not yet.'

'Anyway, you'll never be out of work, there's no shortage of insomniacs.'

'That's true, but, in fact, I have very few patients because I refuse to prescribe sleeping tablets, and a lot of people don't like that. They find pills so reassuring.'

'So what do you do? Sing them lullabies? Tell them bedtime stories?'

'No, but that's what I ought to do. I ought to tell them stories that would wake them up, so that they'd sleep better afterwards. Only I don't have the time because my principal activity is sleep itself.'

She goggled at him in amazement. Joseph cleared his throat, sedately sipped his tea then went on, somewhat ponderously, 'Between men and the truth there lies a gloomy jungle, a jungle with shifting sands, foggy crevasses, flowers that drive you mad, plants that eat time, carnivorous trees and hallucinogenic insects. To reach the truth while avoiding this nightmare forest, men have taken a detour, one that is much less perilous but infinitely longer. This detour is called Reason, and the human caravan has been travelling along it for centuries. But I, I decided to arrive at the truth without following the route of reason. I decided to take a short-cut through the jungle. That's why I sleep, for sleep is this jungle.'

She tossed her head and said with assumed gravity, 'In short, you're an expert on sleep . . . A professional sleeper.'

'More an explorer of sleep, a geographer of dreams. While the mass of mankind is lying deaf and dumb, snoring stupidly, with their noses buried in their pillows, I go down into the deepest abysses of sleep, like a lone speleologist. Einstein said he slept quickly, but I sleep far. And I don't know where I'm going, nor how I'll get back.'

'If I were you, I'd do what Tom Thumb did to be sure of finding

48

his way back to the fold. Moreover, I'd tie myself to my bed with a stout bit of rope, so there'd be no risk of flying away while I was asleep.'

'Oh, I'm not afraid of flying away! On the contrary, when I sleep, flying is my favourite means of locomotion. It's much more practical than walking or going by bike. The world of sleep is so extensive, so deep . . . It's a labyrinth with an infinite number of dimensions, an infinity of possible timescales.'

'Oh, all this talk about time . . . that's right over my head.'

'Well then, imagine a time span that is not fixed. Imagine a clock whose dial is not flat but spherical, and as malleable as a ball of plasticine, a clock whose hands are like snakes biting each other's tails . . .'

'And do you meet anyone else during your excursions between the sheets?'

'Oh, sleep is so vast that there's not much chance of meeting other sleepers. Besides, ordinary dreamers are content to camp prudently outside the cyclopean walls of the Babylon of sleep. They never venture into the unknown. They're nothing but recumbents, small-time sleepers who take no risks. They're not even dreamers, at best they're mere sleepers. They live like tinned beans and snooze like sacks of potatoes. Your real dreamer is a rare bird, too rare for there to be any likelihood of meetings between peers. The deepest levels of sleep are not visited very often, for there's no profit in it. That's why my dreams are solitary. I explore the forbidden city all alone.'

'Ultimately then, what is your sleep – a city or jungle?'

'Let's say it's a city in the heart of the jungle . . . or a jungle in the heart of a city. What's certain is that there's nobody there . . . Except me, walking through the ruins, accompanied by the echo of my footsteps on the cobbles. Nevertheless, I believe I did once meet a true dreamer. I'll never forget him. He was a Spanish monk from the sixteenth century, condemned to the stake by the Inquisition. He was trying to escape from his dungeon through sleep. I can still see him sounding the walls, exploring the staircases, searching desperately for a secret passage that would lead him still further into sleep, in the mad hope that he would not wake up in his prison again. I don't know whether he succeeded. We arranged to meet another night, but sleep is not the best place for making appointments. You can get lost there as easy as winking. In the city of sleep, the streets don't last long and the time of day changes between one door and the next.'

'What you're telling me is a pure cock-and-bull story. There are people who build castles in Spain, but you, you build castles in your bed. Not only are your feet right off the ground, but your head's screwed on back-to-front as well!'

Joseph smiled sadly and said, 'You know, for years and years now I've had to put up with the constant incomprehension of other people, with sly attacks from egotists, gnawing indifference, incessant harassment by idiots, the delight of those who have the power to decide the fate of others but who have no faith left in anything (or who believe in nothing but money, which comes to the same thing), the undermining efforts of disappointed men of all kinds who are jealous of my faith and try to drag me down into the abyss with them. And I have to confront the hedonistic nihilism of some and the unbridled materialism of others . . . I have to put up with all these puppets who busy themselves from morn till night so as to be able to buy themselves more and more gadgets, but who wouldn't lift a finger to save a drowning man. And the worst of all is indifference, because it's faceless, you can't fight it out in the open, though it's everywhere, killing you slowly, by pin-pricks. Even simple people don't understand me, even those I most want to help laugh at me. In the neighbourhood where I live, I hear them whispering behind my back: "Look, Madame Duchnoque, there goes that crackpot from the third floor, you know, the loony doctor who doesn't know whether he's awake or dreaming . . ." And they call me the nut-case, the screwball . . . people wink as I go by. One day, I committed the heinous crime of going out to buy half-a-dozen eggs in my pyjamas. They've never forgiven me, they'd like to persecute me for the rest of my life. As for my dear colleagues, my brother scientists, it's even worse. When I explain that I sleep, not to rest but to explore, they exchange knowing looks and clap me on the back saying, "Oh, bravo, jolly good! Keep up the good work! Chin up, now!" And, in the street, when they see me coming they cross over to the other side. Now, at least *you* will tell me frankly what you think. I'm bonkers, right?'

'Let's say, you have a little bat in your belfry. You're a poet, aren't you? Not my type at all. I like men of action.'

'But I *am* a man of action, damn it! That's what they all refuse to understand! You think dreaming is easy? You think I sleep just for fun? You think a dreamer's life is a bed of roses? I'm a researcher! My bed is my workshop, my laboratory! And a bloody dangerous one at that! God knows how many times I've narrowly escaped leaving my bones to bleach there. Yes, I assure you, I'm risking my life!'

'Under the eiderdown? Well congratulations! But where will these travels in your bed lead you? You'll never make any bread out of your beautiful dreams. That sort of currency is no use except inside your own skull. So, all your knowledge, all your ideas . . . you use them just for sleeping! Whereas you could . . . you could . . . I don't know . . .'

'Make a profit, you mean?'

'And why not? You can't live on dreams and fresh air! Money and fame, that's what counts in life! They bring you dignity and respect. Look at the poor – they walk with their heads hanging, they look at you like beaten dogs, they spend their lives saying, "Yes, sir, No, sir," to their bosses and barking at their wives.'

'Better to walk with your head bowed than to sell your conscience!'

'What use is having a clear conscience if all you can do is gape at the telly in some grotty housing estate and darn your old man's socks while he's down at the bar on the corner, playing cards?'

'I don't like poverty, either, but I'm not out to make money at all costs. I want to do the thing I love, what I think is right, without worrying about whether I lose or gain by it financially. That's my personal idea of luxury. I can't be led by the nose, nor driven with a big stick. I've no intention of kicking myself up the arse all the time, driving myself on like a donkey. Nor do I intend to become the flunkey of my own success, no thank you!'

'All the same, it's social success that earns you other people's respect.'

'No, all you get is other people's attention. That's not the same thing.'

'In any case, I'm sure you can earn money without selling your soul. It's possible to be rich, honest and intelligent.'

'And if I read you correctly, that's what you'd like to meet: a man who's rich, honest and intelligent . . .'

'And courageous. A man who'd love me . . . Well, I can dream, can't I?'

'Yes, but get one thing into your head: if you spend your time hunting high and low for the ideal man, you'll end up with some self-intoxicated clown who'll ditch you as soon as he's got what he wants.'

6

'I did the right thing, shaking her up a bit,' Joseph murmured to himself as he walked through the Jardin des Plantes. If she had even a shadow of feeling for him, she would not hold it against him. Quite the opposite – she would understand clearly that he was not like other men, he was not to be measured by any common yardstick. In a little while, when he had landed the big fish he could already feel nibbling the bait, she would realise that he was no idle visionary drawing maps of the dark side of the moon, nor a layabout slopping around in carpet slippers and living in his own inner world. Soon, she would know what he really was: the Marco Polo of dreams, the Christopher Columbus of sleep!

I like men of action . . . Good for her! There were more than enough to choose from! In these times of spiritual drought, they were the only types you saw about – nonentities in a hurry to climb the ladder of promotion, hyped-up cretins with nimble feet and empty skulls, sporty characters dashing about so as to give the impression they were actually going somewhere . . . *Basta*! Soon, he would hand her the proof of his worth on a silver platter.

Suddenly, he was seized with a desire to work. He decided to go home by way of Léger's library and pick up the promised 'surprise'. It was on the Place du Puits-de-l'Ermite, not far away.

The rain started again just as he was coming out of the Jardin des Plantes. Naturally, he had yet again lost his umbrella.

Limping, for his new shoes hurt his feet, the Christopher Columbus of sleep quickened his pace.

*

The library was deserted. There was only one fat gentleman snoring peacefully at a table, a regular who could only sleep when surrounded by ancient tomes.

Léger had a mania for notices, they were stuck up every-where: CONDEMNED WINDOW, DANGEROUS LADDER, RICKETY TABLE, DO NOT WALK UNDER THIS SHELF . . . In front of the bookshelves was written: BEWARE OF RAT TRAPS. Léger, who liked his solitude and was, moreover, convinced that people came in with the sole purpose of damaging his books, did everything he could to discourage visitors. He was always recounting tales of horrible accidents with books, of skulls fractured by tumbling encyclopedias or lethal dictionaries. Joseph was one of the rare readers whom he welcomed, perhaps because they had something in common: both preferred books to reading.

'Tell me, Léger, what is your opinion of women?' Joseph asked, lighting a cigarette while his friend, stooped like a question mark, brought him an old parchment.

Léger sighed and answered with a weary air, 'They appear to be necessary. But they are harmful to the study of literature. In my view, they should wear the veil, so that the sight of their saucy faces would no longer distract us from our work. (A measure which, let me say, would delight the old and the ugly, that is to say, the majority of women, and would also have the advantage of liberating them all from the rivalry of the flesh, this meat-market to which they are condemned on pain of social ostracism.) Do you think Newton would have discovered the law of gravity if he'd been mooning about women?'

'My dear Léger, we could do without gravity, whereas women . . . Sometimes they are so beautiful . . .'

'Never as beautiful as one of La Rochefoucauld's maxims or a first edition of Cazotte's *Diable amoureux*. Believe me, dear doctor, the pleasure they give us in no way compensates for the torture they inflict. They suck our brains, intrude on our time and disturb our work. In a word, they are nothing but trouble.'

54

'Léger, your extremist view worries me . . .'

'I wonder, dear doctor, whether those of us who wish to devote ourselves entirely to our reading, and enjoy peace of mind – which is, after good health, the supreme blessing – will not eventually be obliged to imitate those Greek cenobites who, with a manly stroke of the knife, boldly cut off their equipment? For you know, nowadays, you can no longer sit down on a bench in the Jardin du Luxembourg, with a fine old tome to read, without one of these creatures passing by, distracting you in mid-sentence by exhibiting some choice morsel of her flesh. And the more brazenly they seem to be offering themselves, the harder they are to get! Frankly, dear doctor, you'd need to be half-blind and have an armour-plated brain to resist this sordid over-sell, this erotic provocation, this frantic display of anything that resembles a bit of arse, all this appetising flesh with which the cinema, the telly and advertising force-feed us so shamelessly. It's as if they were determined to turn us all into lecherous swine! If this is freedom, this constant offering of the cup to one's lips, so that one no longer knows which way to turn, then fuck freedom!'

'It's true,' said Joseph, 'that the more one is free to satisfy one's desires, the more one becomes a slave to them. All the same, women are not to blame for this general decline of everything and everybody regarding what lies below the belt. In fact, they are its first victims.'

'I agree with you, my dear doctor. Today, women are more than ever before compelled to show off their tits to be acceptable to society. Nevertheless, it's true to say they have a natural bent for this kind of thing. Is there a woman alive who dares say to my face that exciting men is *not* her most vital concern? If so, let her throw the first stone!'

Joseph bent his head over the leprous old parchment, written in Latin, which Léger had laid on the table. The latter resumed passionately, 'Women are the stones in our shoes! The thorns in our flesh! Sex is torture and love a Calvary! Ah! If only pleasure didn't exist, how happy we would be!'

'Bloody hell! Have you read this, Léger?'

'No, someone's pinched my Latin dictionary. But I noticed that this manuscript is about sleep. I found it in an old Spanish prayer-book.'

'Listen, I'll translate the bit that's still legible: *To sleep for pleasure is a mortal sin. Just as it is proper for the wife, when visited by her husband, to keep a prayer on her lips while working diligently to satisfy him, so the sleeper carried off by a dream must repeat the name of God in order to fend off the fork-tailed Tempter. For sleep is the door through which the Evil One insinuates himself into the soul. In truth, God never sleeps. That is why I, Lazare Cazal de Papafazar, by the grace of God seventh Grand Inquisitor of Castile, have renounced sleep and all its rites. In the name of the Holy Office I have tracked down adepts of the siesta, somnambulists, hypnotists, those who sleep on their stomachs or with their legs splayed to induce lewd dreams, and all the thrice-damned zealots of sleep. With hatred have I pursued them, and with mercy have I had them burned. In the name of Our Lord have I snatched them from this life of torment. Today, after three years of holy persecution, the land of Castile is as pure as the fleece of the lamb caressed by the hand of Christ resurrected. The fear of God holds sway beneath the arcades of Toledo. However, my work of justice is by no means at an end. I heard it said that a certain monk, a native of Saragossa, had been dabbling in magic. He used to play an enchanted flute from which no sound emerged and which threw into an unholy sleep those who were nightly visited by anxiety and doubt. Instead of forcing them to pray, and chasing away the torments of their souls through mortification of the flesh, he sent them to sleep by means of the melodious silence of his satanic flute. And he said that sleep was good and that the angels loved to sleep. I judged that his words and his acts were impious and I sent the inquisitors to seize him. The iron hand of the Holy Brotherhood fell upon him. The fra redemptors lovingly made his bones crack to exhort him to the proper worship of God. In the name of the Holy Office I granted him atonement by fire. But, on the day of the Auto da Fé, his lifeless* body was found in the in pace, *where he had been awaiting the beneficial fire. The priors say he is burning in Hell, but I know that his soul was able to escape by means of some diabolical artifice, for he said to me, as he groaned upon the rack, that sleep would save him . . .'*

'That's the monk in my dream!' thought Joseph, 'But, good God, can this be true?'

'Go on, doctor, go on,' said Léger impatiently.

'Yes . . . *I know that this heretical monk has escaped from the redeeming fire throughout the labyrinths of infamous sleep. I know that in the pagan principalities of sleep he is tempting the spirits of sleepers and that he has carnal commerce with the souls of sleeping women. All this I judge to be an impiety and I have resolved to put an end to it. I have determined to travel in the lower depths of dreams and there to search for the heretical monk. Thus, I have slept in the name of Our Lord, kissing the crucifix and angels have appeared unto me. And they have commanded me to pursue the work of the Holy Inquisition in the States of Sleep and to exterminate in the name of God all those ungodly ones who take refuge there to escape the eye of Our Lord, and all those lascivious sleepers who indulge in dreams out of a taste for the voluptuous. I, Lazare Cazal de Papafazar, by the grace of God seventh Grand Inquisitor of Castile, have received a mission from the perfumed lips of angels to punish those who travel in dreams to gather forbidden fruit and to learn spells that will serve to deliver the world into the hands of the Prince of Darkness. In the name of God, the angels have named me Bishop of Sleep. And I have made a vow to sleep zealously until such time as the Spirit of Deceit shall be annihilated from the realms of sleep. And I shall leave this body of mine, which is gnawed by an ulcer, not through death but through sleep, a realm where Time does not exist. Inspired by the wrath of God, armed by the angels and guided by a holy hatred of Evil, I will plant the standard of the Holy Office upon the plain of dreams, and I will eradicate from sleep all its evil devotees, its lustful dreamers, its sorcerers and magicians. In the name of God will I sleep until*

57

the Apocalypse. Then my soul, sated with carnage, its wrath appeased and its hatred satisfied, will fly to join Our Lord in the highest heavens where, amidst the glory that is my due, I will enjoy myself throughout eternity.'

Out in the streets, amidst the shouts of the dustmen, Joseph again felt exhilarated, as if he were standing on a mountain peak.

Reaching home, he put on his finest pyjamas (a ceremonial Tibetan pair) and, with his slippers on his feet, began to pace round his dreamery, letting out little chuckles of excitement. He felt that his mind was blazing with light. The least of his gestures was an expression of pure genius. His eyes perceived the sublime hidden in every object. It seemed to him that the power of his brain was limitless, capable of reducing mountains to dust and of subjugating the entire human race. He felt himself to be a Titan of thought destined for universal glory. He would have liked Sonia to be there to witness his splendour. He looked at himself in the mirror. His eyes were glittering, he looked like a madman. The cat, sprawled across a 25-volume edition of *La Comédie humaine*, was watching him with a pained expression.

Joseph, wanting Livingstone to share his exaltation, ran into the kitchen and opened a tin of sardines. The cat, without waiting for an invitation or seeking an explanation, attacked the sardines. Joseph, in a sudden access of tenderness, stroked him gently.

'You'll see,' he said, 'one day, we'll go *down there*. You're a true Parisian, born in the Père-Lachaise cemetery, but you'll like it *down there*, I'm sure . . . You've never seen a goat, have you? They're nice creatures, goats . . . And then, you know, the mice down there don't run so fast as they do here, they go *pianu pianu* . . .'

But the cat, feeling the caresses somehow threatened his sardines, started to growl.

'Ugh, you villain!' said Joseph, 'you don't growl at me when I give you rice pudding, do you? Sardines are too good for you, they make you evil-tempered!'

He went back into the dreamery, opened the window overlooking the courtyard and inhaled a deep lungful of air. Behind the window opposite, the fossil apartment still kept its secrets under lock and key. By the light of the moon, Joseph thought he could make out some sort of chest . . . what could it contain?

He lit a cigarette and began to jog up and down on the spot. Too many ideas were churning in his head. He felt the need of movement. 'Let's hope I'm not ill,' he said to himself.

He was as worked up as if he had found the map of a buried treasure without being able to decipher it. He decided to listen to a little music, to calm himself. The trouble was, all his records reminded him of moments of exhaustion and despair. Then he thought of the old jazz record, which he had not yet played.

He took his pocket torch and went down into the cellar to fetch his ancient record-player.

A few minutes later, the antique 78 was sputtering and crackling on the dusty turntable. Because of the title, *Sleep Party*, Joseph was expecting to hear a very slow piece, a kind of lullaby.

It did, in fact, begin very gently.

But little by little the rhythm hotted up. Picking up speed, it went faster and faster, like a train pulling out of a station.

The acceleration, regular at first, became more and more feverish and anarchic. It was as if the various instruments were chasing each other, and gradually this runaway pursuit made them lose their heads, they became delirious, bolted full speed ahead, their feet no longer touching the ground, as if the devil was at their heels – and, all of a sudden, it was as if they had imploded, trampling, splitting, exterminating and devouring each other in a frenzied and hallucinatory cacophony. The musicians seemed to be trying to disembowel Time, to strangle it with the strings, crush it with a great clash of cymbals, suffocate it with trumpets and trombones. It sounded like a concert given by an orchestra of demented children. It gave Joseph the impression that he was on a toboggan, sliding down towards oblivion. It was a primordial music, the primaeval hubbub, the racket you hear in your mother's womb or at the heart of the sun. It was the sound of stellar collisions, sidereal explosions and black holes. It was the music of the treadmill of Time, the music of the great Wheel of the cosmos, the music of the merry-go-round of the universe. It was the laughter of matter itself.

After listening to it several times, Joseph had to yield to the evidence: in spite of – or perhaps because of – its frantic tempo, the music possessed an undeniably soporific power. The mind lost its foothold, was seized with vertigo, longed to let go, to be carried away by this sonorous torrent, to be annihilated in this musical gibberish, this supraterrestrial hullabaloo.

It occurred to Joseph to try playing it again, but turning the volume down progressively. It seemed to him this augmented the soporific effect. He looked at Livingstone. The cat, rolled up into a ball on Montaigne's *Essays*, was sleeping like a dormouse.

Joseph went over and tickled his stomach. Livingstone began to purr.

'Oh, you, you're so laid back!' said Joseph, 'you take life in your stride . . . Ah, if only I, too, could purr, instead of knocking my brains out, how soothing it would be . . .'

He froze on the spot, thunderstruck by what he had just said. Then he slapped his forehead with the palm of his hand, exclaiming, 'God's teeth, that's it, of course! Purring is a preliminary to sleep! All rhythm is soothing, but the intensity of the sound stimulates the nervous system! The cat's lulled by his own purring because he hears it with his body, not with his ears . . . And that monk who sent people to sleep with a silent flute! Why, sweet Jesus, that's it, for sure! To produce a soporific effect, the rhythm must be perceived by the brain without stimulating the ear! And to achieve that, there's only one possibility: translate it into supersonic sound!'

The shock of this discovery caused Joseph to sit down abruptly on the bed. Stunned, he gaped at the alarm clock without seeing it. Then suddenly his attention was riveted to the dial. He had just remembered his dream: 'It's not an alarm clock, it's a sleep-machine.'

He jumped to his feet. In his ceremonial pyjamas, he linked his hands above his head and did a kind of Tahitian belly-dance.

It was a dance of victory

The cat watched him without a hint of astonishment.

After a few minutes of these solemn contortions, Joseph stood beside his bed and proclaimed to the pillow, 'In the name of humanity, I, Joseph Cavalcanti, take possession of the Empire of Sleep and, furthermore, establish my government, my authority and my jurisdiction over all the provinces of dreams and all adjoining territories.'

Part Two

1

Felix Rapion put his golf club to his shoulder, closed one eye and, through the bay-window, took aim at the four-engined jet that had just taken off from Orly Airport. It was the 16.27 Paris–Tokyo flight.

'Rat-a-tat-tat-rat-a-tat-tat!' he growled furiously.

He had, he decided, scored a direct hit. The aircraft was about to flatten a block of council flats. He put his golf club on his desk, picked up the telephone, dialled a number and barked, 'Rapion here. How's it going? . . . 'Flu, 'flu, what's that supposed to mean? Either you're dead or alive, man, there's no in-between! Get out of the office for a while, come down to the factory! The atmosphere in Paris is foul, you need some oxygen. This is just the moment, everything's in bud, the sun is shining, planes are crashing, cars are ramming each other up the backside, long live spring! . . . Right, now listen, your so-called plans for launching the *Dreamboat* programme, you can stick them up your arse. God's holy whorehouse! It isn't as if I didn't explain it all clearly to you! Simple, mindless sleep is out! Finished, out-of-date, kaput! Consumers don't want to sleep like dumbbells nowadays, or like cows in a field, they want a better class of sleep, an up-market, more profitable sleep! So our campaign has to be zingy and full of pep! For example, I'd like to see a badge on sale in chemists' shops: *Put a tiger in your pillow*! Well, you get the picture. Consumers need a "plus" in their sleep. The product must be aimed at people who sleep normally but have a legitimate ambition to sleep better than the Joneses. Egalitarianism in sleep, that's old hat. It's not right that a man who has made a success in life should not be able to afford a better sleep than some poor jerk who's out of work. As for him, thanks to *Dreamboat*, even he'll be in a position to enjoy the luxury of a top-executive sleep. The *Dreamboat* project will give everyone the feeling of belonging to an élite, of being different from the masses. As for the promotional campaign, I want it everywhere, even in village pharmacies. Remember, it was the farmers who made our *Narcogoldor* such a success. They're very demanding, life in the fields has become a jungle. So, get with it, boy, all systems go, we've got to be in there fighting on all fronts. In the towns people need sleeping pills because of the noise, in the country they need them to make the silence bearable. And as for sensitising the doctors, find some new angle for me. Doctors are intellectuals, you have to suck up to them tactfully. Maybe we could offer the most deserving a plane ticket for the sales conference on sleep we're going to organise this summer . . . only, if it takes place in Düsseldorf or Zagreb, they'll make paper darts out of the tickets. Where, then . . . Tahiti? Yes, that's an idea. A conference in Tahiti, all expenses paid, with *vahinas* laid on, that could motivate them. It's in our interest to make them dream, so's they'll make their patients sleep well . . . Eh? Well, you mustn't despair, ideas will come to you as you work on it. You know, when you're sick, you're not such an arse-hole. Good, you'll work all that out for me, then, get it perfect . . . Ah, yes! And while I think of it, do me a favour and renew our livestock. We need some new girl canvassers, some fresh tits. The doctors must associate our pills with rosy thoughts. Never forget that tits are the best promotional aid there is. Our sleeping-pills are young, dynamic products, heralds of hope and the future. Our clientèle no longer consists of nervous old biddies who can't sleep, it includes everybody, even dogs and children. So we need to be bright and breezy, full of the joys of living! Faith alone will save us! Right, that'll be all for today. And don't forget to take some fresh air. Jump out of the window, it'll do you good!'

Felix Rapion hung up and swivelled his office chair round to face the bay window. He looked out with pride upon the little garden he had had laid out between the parking lot and the factory laboratory. 'Pity there aren't any birds,' he said to himself, 'that would make it nicer. I'll buy half a dozen. They can't cost much.'

In the sunny yard in front of the laboratory, a group of engineers in white overalls were standing around smoking. Felix Rapion was indignant. 'What do I pay these layabouts for?' He picked up his golf club and aimed.

At that moment, the intercom buzzed. 'Excuse me, sir,' said a shrill female voice, 'that man who insists on seeing you personally is here again . . .'

'That nut who rings up in the middle of the night?'

'Yes, sir. Shall I tell him you're in a meeting?'

'No, send him in, it'll be relaxing.'

A few moments later, the individual in question came into the office. He was armed with an umbrella, in spite of the fine spring sunshine, and hugged a leather briefcase lovingly against his chest. Casting an uneasy glance at the green plant as he passed, he moved forward across the wall-to-wall carpet cautiously, as if suspecting it were mined. He was of medium height, his greying hair was in need of a comb, his face was ravaged and there were bags under his eyes. His sombre looks were at once stern and naif, stamped with an unfathomable sadness that was crossed now and then by the fleeting light of a fanatical conviction. There was something of Buster Keaton about him, but of Buster at the end of his tether. His crumpled raincoat was beyond hope, his tie an object of horror, half verdigris and half goose-shit. Looking at him, it was hard to decide whether he had never managed to get any sleep or had never managed to wake up. He seemed completely out of phase, under the weather, but it was evident that he was making superhuman efforts to appear normal.

'Very good day, sir, director,' he stammered, 'Or rather, I mean: good morning, Mr President . . . Er . . . I am . . .'

'Dr Cavalcanti, yes, my secretary gave me your card.' He

pointed to an armchair with his golf club. 'Take a seat, please. What can I do for you?'

Joseph, clutching the arm-rests, lowered himself gingerly into the armchair, as if afraid it was about to swallow him up. Then, all in one breath, having obviously learned his speech by heart, he declared: 'I know your time is precious, so I will come straight to the point. I have just been to the Patents Office to register an apparatus I have invented and which, I believe, might be of interest to you. It is a supersonic diffuser with soporific properties. It produces a special repetitive rhythm, translated into supersonic waves, with the aim of being perceptible to the brain without exciting the tympani or mobilising the conscious attention. This ultra-sonic rhythm, short-circuiting the ear, thus acts directly on the unconscious . . .'

Felix Rapion, toying with his golf club, listened without batting an eyelid. Joseph opened his briefcase and brought out a contraption that looked like an alarm clock, except that the dial, which was devoid of hands and numbers, was as full of holes as Gruyère cheese. It was the Soviet alarm clock transformed into a sleep-inducing machine.

'Here is the prototype,' Joseph went on. 'You wind it up like a conventional alarm, but one could of course make an electric model. As for the results of its experimental use, here they are.'

He took out a dossier and went on, 'These experiments were carried out at the La Salpêtrière Hospital on a sample of one hundred insomniacs. While the most effective sleeping tablets induced sleep in 73% of subjects within the first half-hour after ingestion, I obtained a success rate of 87% with the Sleepmaker (that's what I call my invention). Moreover, using it does not cause the slightest physical or mental disturbance, nor is there any phenomenon of addiction. I may add that the cost of production would be derisory.'

Felix Rapion contemplated the Gruyère alarm clock, which Joseph had placed on his desk, with curiosity. But he did not touch it.

68

'It's the opposite of an alarm clock, in effect,' he said in a mildly ironic tone. 'Instead of waking you up, it sends you to sleep. Instead of telling the time, it tells . . . eternity.' Then, suddenly, with an affectedly worried air, 'But isn't there a risk of never waking up again?'

'Of course not,' replied Joseph. 'The length of time the Sleepmaker functions can be varied to suit the user. Thus, instead of an alarm set to go off at seven a.m., one can set the Sleepmaker to stop at seven a.m. Besides, my machine does not induce a comatose sleep. It helps you to sleep, but in no way does it hinder your waking up.'

'Well then, my dear doctor, I congratulate you,' declared Felix Rapion, 'your sleep-inducing alarm clock is an extraordinary machine! I am convinced it will have a prodigious success . . . a few centuries from now. As for myself, what would you have me do with it? Do you want me to announce to my shareholders that sleeping pills are out of date? Would you like me to tell my eight thousand employees to go and fry fish, because I've decided to recycle myself into a manufacturer of sleep-inducing alarm clocks, which will bring me in just about enough money to buy a one-wheeled bicycle? Now, I'm going to tell you frankly what I think of your invention, because I've taken a liking to you. I like idealists. I, too, am an idealist – but only at the weekend. Listen, Dr Cavalcanti, your Sleepmaker is purely Utopian. Why? Quite simply because it will not bring in any profit to compensate for the losses it will cause.'

Nervously, Joseph ploughed a furrow in the carpet with the tip of his umbrella. 'I came to you first and foremost because I thought your essential concern was to help people sleep,' he said. 'I see I was wrong. All I can do is take myself and my invention elsewhere. For example, to a manufacturer of electrical and domestic appliances.'

'Good idea! But you'll draw a blank. Setting up and promoting these innovations costs the eyes out of your head. Your contraption for sending people bye-byes cannot be integrated into an existing structure, we'd need new factories to manufacture it, special distribution networks, people specially trained to sell it . . . Your Sleepmaker would not begin to show a profit for ten years. Ten years, in the life of a financier is . . . it's Never-Never-Land! In ten years, if the world still exists, I may be selling concrete or socks or publishing books. At the present moment of speaking, the banks' computers can't even predict what's going to happen in six months, so, just imagine, ten years. . . ! Today, it's only the short term that counts. Navigate within sight of land, that's the order of the day. Make as much money as you possibly can, as fast as you can. The rest is for the birds. The "future" and all that ballyhoo, that's just a gimmick to put one over on the public . . . Well, doctor, you're not a fool, you know what the score is.'

Felix Rapion smiled at seeing Joseph crushed. How delightful, for a self-made man, to be able to give an intellectual a lesson on life! It was for moments like this that, for years, he had kept slogging away on the treadmill.

He took a delight in driving the sword in deeper, giving Joseph the *coup de grâce*: 'Besides,' he said, 'let us suppose your Sleepmaker actually succeeded in threatening part of my market. I'd simply manufacture the same thing, but square instead of round, and undercut your retail price by ten per cent. No, believe me, your sleep-alarm is not made for this day and age. It's too clever by half.'

A long silence followed these words. Then Joseph suddenly exclaimed, 'And what about people in all this rigmarole, what about them? Don't they have any say, all these people who are poisoning themselves with sleeping pills? Swallowing tablets in the belief that they are protecting their health, whereas, in reality, they're protecting nothing but the health of the pharmaceutical industry? It doesn't matter if they drop dead, does it, just so long as the chemists are doing fine!'

Felix Rapion pointed his golf club at Joseph: 'Dr Cavalcanti, I'm no philosopher. What I do, more modestly, is provide a livelihood

70

for thousands of families by giving people work. My aim in life is not to have beautiful ideas, but to develop my enterprise and make a contribution to progress.'

'Has it never occurred to you that true progress is not making ever-more-effective sleeping pills, but finding a way to make people lead healthy lives, so that they can sleep soundly? Have you ever thought that silence, pure air and nature are much more vital to man than the progress of chemistry? Have you never realised that it is impossible to overcome loneliness, stress, ugliness and pollution with pills?'

'Now hold on a minute, young man! I'm not responsible for the fate of the human race! I didn't shit the world out of my arse! People want to sleep, so I make sleeping pills. If they wanted to shove feathers up their backsides, I'd breed ostriches. You're a dreamer, Dr Cavalcanti, you understand nothing about men. They have no desire to gather raspberries or listen to the nightingale, they want to sit besotted in front of the telly, roast themselves on polluted beaches, drive about in their cars and swallow pretty pills. Why? Because they are pricks by nature. A glow-worm will always seem to them more wonderful that a star. Men are children who must be given toys. They like shiny things, new things, useless things. Offer them the maxims of Confucius, they'll wipe their arses on them. Give them a painted turd, they'll put it in a showcase. Just look at them!' (He aimed his golf club in the direction of Paris.) 'There they are, crouched in their cars in the middle of a traffic jam, listening to the Pastoral Symphony on their magnificent stereo car radios, and they're happy because they believe they're freer than the people crushed into the metro trains! And those poor devils, squashed like sardines in a tin, are happy too, because, when they look at the advertisements with palm-trees and naked women on them, they think they're freer than the Zulu snoozing in his hammock! The truth is, they're masochists. They love to be crushed. They were made for it, the way sheep are made to be shorn of their wool and eaten.'

'Monsieur Rapion,' Joseph answered, his eyes glittering, his hands convulsively clutching his umbrella, 'you remind me of that Gestapo officer who forced his prisoners to live in their own excrement so as to prove to them they were nothing but pigs. You and your kind put men into cages and, when they turn vicious through being shut up, deduce that they deserve to be in cages. But if men are stupid, it's because they've been treated like idiots, if they're bad, it's because they've felt the big stick, if they're hypocrites it's because they've been duped by show-men's patter, by illusionists and fortune-tellers . . . In any case, let's hope that the politicians, industrialists, technocrats, finan-ciers and generals who decide our fate do not share your contempt for the human race, because if so – '

'You make me laugh, Dr Cavalcanti! You come to me to sell a somniferous machine and, when I refuse it, you start preaching morality! Just because you haven't been able to palm off your cheapjack gadget, you get on your high horse and play the prophet! If you knew how to make a bit of loot, you'd be a little less concerned about the fate of mankind!'

'If I don't know how to "make a bit of loot", as you put it, it's because I've always preferred to follow my dreams, rather than split my skull calculating what I could gain, and fret myself sick with worrying about what I might lose. I consider that to live solely for material interests is not interesting. And, in the end, it doesn't even pay.'

'If you really believe what you say, you're a pure soul and I take my hat off to you. But that's all I can do for you. I reckon you don't have a chance. When you want to do something new, you have to have the look of a killer. You, I'm afraid, are nothing but a visionary heading for obscurity. You imagine that men will recognise your greatness of soul, but they'll always judge you by the colour of your tie. If you want to make them happy, good luck to you, but here's a piece of advice: make your will first, because they'll get you for sure. Approach them without shield or weapon, and they'll certainly attack you. Open their eyes for them, they will gouge yours out. Show them their folly, they will send you to the madhouse. Give them a whiff of sincerity, they will cry "Halloo!" and hunt you like a fox. Offer them your love, they will use you for a dartboard. As for women, let's not speak of them! If you have nothing to offer them but the truth, they will avoid you like the plague!'

Joseph stood up and said. 'You believe that all mankind resembles your subordinates, but allow me to disabuse you. There still exist men worthy of the name, men who will never sit up and beg, who will not sell their brothers for the sake of a cosy niche in life. It's true they take a little finding,' (he began scratching the carpet with the tip of his umbrella) 'but they exist, believe me, they exist! And it is for them that I have created my machine!'

Felix Rapion stood up in his turn and said, 'Well, I hope that, if you keep on digging, you'll find these underground men of yours, and that they'll agree to invest their money in your toy. And now, I won't detain you any longer.'

Joseph, his lips trembling with suppressed rage, picked up his Sleepmaker, put it back in his briefcase and made for the door. But, before crossing the threshold, he turned back. 'There's one thing it's impossible to control at will, Monsieur Rapion, and that is one's own conscience. You may think you know all the tunes but you yourself are no more than a simple instrument. You partake of the feast, but you are also an item on the menu. My regards to your family.'

From his bay-window, Felix Rapion watched Joseph's slight silhouette crossing the parking lot, leaving by the factory gates and turning towards the station. 'That seedy bastard doesn't even own a car,' thought the Managing Director. 'Featherbrains like him are good for nothing but shovelling chickenshit. Those who oppose progress should be strangled at birth.' He turned his eyes towards the long procession of vehicles, jammed together on the ring road in the light of the setting sun. 'The problem is, there are too many of us. Far too many. We ought to be able to introduce a system of selection. Be free to eliminate all those who drag their feet and slow down the march of humanity. It's so exhausting, having to kick people up the arse all the time to make them advance . . . Ah, well, in a few years' time, I'll have enough to buy my desert island. No more paperwork, no more telephones, no more trade unions, no more nothing. A natural life. Ah, what a luxury!'

The telephone rang. He picked it up. 'Yes? . . . What!? They're insisting that we limit the *ganachoramollicin* to seven per cent? The swine! They know perfectly well we've always got eighteen months' supply in stock! Just because some baboon has kicked the bucket in a Health Department lab, they want to make us lose two billion! . . . No, don't try to sweet-talk them. If the other lot get in at the next election, we could be in trouble. It'd be better to try and offload the stock, on the quiet, from now on. See what the export department can come up with. Maybe we can find a buyer in Ugambia. Get hold of Colonel Kandodo, he's the Minister of something or other. We've been on safari together . . . he's a good sort . . . OK, keep me up-to-date.'

He hung up and continued his meditations, playing with the golf club: 'That's what that nutcase of a doctor didn't understand – if you want to get off the treadmill, you have to make it spin still faster . . .'

He smiled, pleased with his imagery. But the smile turned into a grimace. That pain in his stomach had come back.

2

For Joseph, the days that followed were a Via Dolorosa.

At first, he thought that, in Rapion, he had had the misfortune to run up against a rare cretin, a narrow mind blinkered by obsessive commercialism. He was convinced that any business-man with common sense would immediately be interested in his Sleepmaker. But he was quickly brought down to earth. Most of the industrialists he tried to contact would not even see him. For the sake of his invention, he had to do the rounds like any common salesman of office supplies and touch his forelock to harassed secretaries who, out of spite, took delight in sending him packing. He was often thrown out like a tramp. One Head of Department laughed till he cried when he saw Joseph's invention. The only power all these penpushers had was the power to say 'No,' and they gloried in it. It was their revenge for everything. Declaring, in a voice of hypocritical regret, 'I'm so sorry but we can't . . .' gave them the feeling of being a little more alive, the impression of belonging to the élite. They were watch-dogs. They were not permitted to enter the master's house, but they had the satisfaction of preventing others from approaching it. And they spent their lives sucking on this miserable little tyranny, their one luxury, as if sucking marrow out of a bone.

The bankers, on the other hand, were extremely affable with Joseph. Not one was grudging of his time and they all took pains to demonstrate that, owing to A and B, just at the present moment, and given the economic contingencies, it was only possible to invest in products which had already proved

75

themselves on the export markets. Before deciding on an investment, they had to be sure of the short-term return. They advised him to continue his research within the framework of an established enterprise, with the aim of directing his work more specifically towards 'current market imperatives'. And then they shook hands, offering him plenty of encouragement and beaming their well-oiled smiles. Ah! The day would come when their blindness would blow their brains out, and their courteous indifference would freeze the blood in their veins!

Joseph, his head bowed and his heart blazing with rage, went home and threw himself on the bed. *'Disgraziatu!'* he growled, burrowing his head into the pillow. It was too awful, too unjust . . . How could these undersized manikins, not worthy to clean his shoes, decide his fate? And to think that he had already seen himself travelling round the world, lecturing on dreams, triumphantly sending his audiences to sleep . . . He could picture himself presiding over a faculty of sleep, with thousands of students of Dreams dreaming in giant dormitories, each with a mission to bring back nuggets of truth from his sleep . . . Like a new Cortés at the head of an army of sleepers, he would have delivered to a dazzled world the El Dorado of dreams . . . He would have known glory . . . had breakfast in bed every morning . . .

And now, oblivion! He, the king of sleep, was the victim of a lot of nonentities and little money-grubbers, subjected to the rule of a legion of mummies determined to stultify all sources of life, all enthusiasm, all faith, all the genius that came within their range! It was enough to make you bang your head against the wall!

Sitting under the portrait of Christopher Columbus, the cat contemplated Joseph with a cold and resigned eye. Today would not be a sardine day.

During these cold dark days, full of rebuffs and humiliations, Joseph lost two kilos, three umbrellas and all his illusions. He was seized with profound disgust for the human race. But, very quickly, he realised that this would be to give Rapion best and adopt his contemptible point of view. Only a pig thinks all men are swine.

Rapion, that omnipotent, dishonest shopkeeper, capable of selling the world and its future for twopence, made him feel utterly sick. He manufactured sleeping pills as if they were jelly-babies for children, but he himself was unwittingly drawn into the general infantilisation. He laughed at his fellow-men, without seeing that he himself was a puppet in the hands of Satan.

'To lose one's illusions gently, without sinking into despair, that is the serious business of life,' said Joseph to himself, 'and the greatest illusion is imagining that one can be more than other men, more than a man, more than a simple parenthesis in flesh and blood between nothingness and nothingness. One can avoid becoming a dog or a monkey, one cannot succeed in becoming a god. There is nothing to be got out of life, absolutely nothing. But there is plenty one can give. Only what we give becomes definitively ours.'

When evening fell, Joseph, full of bitter ruminations, made his way to the *Amis du Sport*. He went there for Sonia's sake. Not in the hope of seeing her, but to restore his morale with a few glasses of white wine and so give himself the Dutch courage to ring her. He had not seen her since that day at the Museum. He had spent the winter perfecting his Sleepmaker and, during all that time, he had been so convinced of his imminent success that he had preferred to wait for fame and fortune before contacting the young woman again. What to do now? He longed to see her and tell her all. If she did not understand, well then, *basta*! So much the worse for her, and so much the worse for him! He would blow his brains out, and so goodnight! The comedy would be over, he would ring down the curtain.

Only, after knocking back two or three glasses of wine to give himself the courage to 'phone, he found he had the courage not to. Right. He had lost the battle, but not the war. The fact that none of these conformist midgets was interested in his invention was, precisely, the proof that it was a work of genius. Twisted minds appreciate only what is twisted. Monkeys would rather have a banana than a diamond. He had cast a pearl before swine, that was the long and short of it. And, anyway, the failure of his Sleepmaker was not the end of the world – there were still so many things to dream about . . .

With his glass in front of him, Joseph sought consolation by reminding himself that it had taken Christopher Columbus twenty years of effort before anyone had deigned to grant him a vessel, whereas any sycophantic courtier had only to do a few *ronds de jambes* to get what he wanted in twenty seconds.

The *patron*, meanwhile, was polishing his brand-new coffee-maker (an ultra-modern machine studded with chrome knobs), or serving balloon glasses of red wine to the retired civil servants who were playing *belote*. From the exalted height of his Stalin moustache, he dominated the little world, spouting maxims in a telling manner or firing shafts of wit that spared nothing and nobody. Passages of purple prose alternated with eloquent silences, pompous discourses gave way to laconic humour, devastating satire succeeded sublime and lyrical flights of fancy. Between one *pastis* and the next, he solved all the problems of the world. His counter was his soap-box, from which he reigned as an enlightened despot over a few square metres of the planet.

One evening when he was lying in ambush under the rows of liqueur bottles, just waiting for a victim to harangue, a fire engine dashed by with its siren screaming. Tossing his drying-up cloth over his shoulder, he began applauding ostentatiously, peeping out of the corner of his eye to see the effect of his gesture. The *belote*-players, having reached a critical point in their game, did not even look up. Only Joseph, out of courtesy, raised an eyebrow in a vague interrogative. This was all The Father of the People needed and he began to declaim, waving the drying-up cloth to give dramatic emphasis. 'Somewhere, blood is flowing, the firemen go by and I applaud. Yes, I confess, I did applaud. You are asking yourself what my gesture signifies, and I understand your perplexity. I want you to know, monsieur, that I was not applauding the disaster. I was applauding the firemen. They wade through blood, they scrape up bits of brain from the murderous asphalt with a teaspoon, they hold the hand of the despairing man who no longer believes in anything, because nobody believes in him, they cut down the hanged, they fling themselves into the flames to rescue the infant sobbing in his cradle, they climb along slippery roofs, at peril of their lives, to rescue the reckless cat who has ventured too far. However, observe them: health, good sense and dynamic energy beam from their faces. Why, you ask me? Because they are conscious of being useful to others! Because they enjoy the esteem of their fellow-citizens! Because the people need them! Because they give of themselves without thought of profit!'

He poured himself another glass of red, took a great swig, cleared his throat and resumed: 'Their unbounded devotion and their silent abnegation spare them from the moral ravages that the assiduous practice of egoism and cowardice induce among many of us. Their fresh complexions, their jolly laughter and their love of the bottle are proof that only the sense of duty fends off apprehension and ensures joy in living. Verily, verily I say unto you: Only the firemen shall be saved! Those who rush into the flames shall emerge glowing with light! As for those who turn away from the catastrophe, or pretend not to see it, woe betide them, for they shall be consumed from within!'

'Nowadays,' remarked one of the card-players who had been listening with half an ear, 'being useful to others has become a luxury. *Belote* and *rebelote*. My great-nephew, now, he wanted to join the fire brigade, but they gave him to understand that he'd have to be the son of a fireman. It seems "fireman" is a hereditary title. Result: my great nephew set fire to his classroom. Ten of trumps.'

'There you are, that's an admirable proof of my thesis,' said The Father of the People, 'prevent a bloke from becoming a fireman and he turns into a pyromaniac!'

'I didn't say that,' objected the card-player, 'he's not a

pyromaniac, my great-nephew, he just sets fire to things, that's all.'

The Father of the People went on: 'To ensure that nobody is deprived of the satisfaction of serving others, we should all become firemen. Writers would be firemen of the mind, owners of bars would be firemen of the gullet, women firemen of the cock . . .'

Joseph could not help laughing.

'Bravo, monsieur,' said The Father of the People, 'your jaws unlock, you become a philosopher. God created the universe in a burst of laughter. He who seeks the truth with a frown on his face and his chin in his hand is as ridiculous as a monkey looking for his fleas with a telescope. The spirit of seriousness is always self-deluding. It's not humour that distorts things, it's solemnity. A sense of humour is a sense of life. Life is essentially a comedy.'

'And do you think there was something comical about the gas-chambers?' asked Joseph.

The *patron* parried the thrust. 'If the Nazis had had a sense of humour, would they have built gas-chambers? If they'd had a sense of humour, they wouldn't have been Nazis in the first place. Believe me, the spirit of seriousness has done more harm than cholera and the plague put together.'

'And death,' said Joseph, 'isn't that sad?'

The Father of the People drained his glass and declared gravely, 'Anything that separates me from the Inspector of Inland Revenue can't be all bad.'

'Got you!' cried one of the *belote*-players viciously as he slapped a card down on the table. 'Eh, there, Father of the People, make me a small espresso. We're about to board the enemy ship!'

Then he rammed his Basque beret on his head, ready for battle, and prophesied through clenched teeth, 'There will be butchery . . .'

The faces of the card-players, as they picked up and tossed down their cards with emphatic little flourishes, portrayed the whole gamut of human expression: anxiety, fatuous disdain, humility, resignation, dejection, rage, hatred, magnanimity in the moment of triumph . . . In this microcosm, this image of life, they revealed its grotesque character, its absurd alternation between hope and disappointment, success and failure. You win, you lose, you win, you lose, you win, you lose and, finally, you leave the arena.

Suddenly, the new coffee-machine emitted a strident whistle and started churning out coffee as if there was no tomorrow. Boiling water spurted in all directions. The Father of the People pressed all the knobs in a frantic effort to regain control of his runaway machine.

'Is this a revolution?' asked one of the card-players imperturbably. 'Should we go down to the air-raid shelter?'

'Perhaps we should call the fire brigade,' said another ironically.

The Father of the People, his moustache covered in froth, his nose spattered with the drops of scalding coffee that were squirting all over the place, screwed up his eyes against the jets of steam, picked up a bottle and started hitting his machine like a madman.

At last, the exhausted coffee-maker, after a few more hiccups and a final agonised shriek, stopped dead, vanquished by the ingenuity of man.

'Phew!' sighed The Father of the People, wiping his forehead. 'All things considered, I should have kept the old one. It was more work, but at least I understood how it functioned. I didn't have butterflies in my stomach every time I had to make coffee. With this brute, the slightest error is fatal. The boffin who invented this infernal machine thought of everything, except that the people who use it aren't robots.' And, addressing himself to Joseph, who was preparing to leave, 'The chaps who invent things should pay a bit more attention to their brain-children . . . Hey! You've left your umbrella!'

*

Joseph went home. He felt better. He always recovered a little towards nightfall.

As soon as he got in, he started pacing up and down his dreamery with a fag in his mouth. In his head, he was ranging round and round like a tiger in a cage. He was thinking as intensely – and as vainly – as a man condemned to death. He was trying to seize hold of certain ideas. He told himself that a man's greatness is measured by his capacity to endure misfortune. And that, in order to have a chance of being happy, one must renounce happiness once and for all. He told himself that only suffering can bring peace of mind and only failure can soften the idea of death. These were great and true thoughts. The trouble was, Joseph would gladly have exchanged these great and true thoughts for the faculty of ceasing to think altogether.

However, there was nothing doing. He could not switch off his head as he could the electric current. His brain functioned blindly, stupidly, it had no brakes and could turn against its proprietor as the infernal machine at the *Amis du Sport* had done. Today, his mind was taking its revenge for the way he had abused it. For years he had driven it like an overworked donkey, now he must take the consequences.

The cat, stretched out on the bed, was sleeping the sleep of the just. Joseph lit another cigarette and set to cudgelling his brains once more like a damned soul. He was knitting his synapses, pedalling the treadmill of his brain, feverishly kneading his grey matter, and driving himself crazy.

The recollection of all his past hopes weighed on him like a tombstone.

And if he were to put a bullet through his skull? Soonest done, soonest mended? There was a loaded revolver in the drawer of his desk. The thing would be over in a moment, just enough time to say 'ouch'. . .

He turned towards Livingstone, who had woken up and was glaring at him fiercely.

'Yes, you're right,' said Joseph, 'better to have a little snifter of cognac.'

Which he did.

He felt no desire to go to bed. The night brings counsel, nobody knew that better than he did but, lately, sleep had brought him nothing but tacky nightmares, plodding dreams that were not worth the detour. Ever since he had started work on his Sleepmaker the previous autumn, Joseph had had little leisure to concentrate on his sleep. Like any Sunday dreamer, he had scamped his nights, sleeping without any proper sequence to his ideas.

What time was it? Barely nine. An empty evening was beginning, the prelude to an endless night. He felt he ought to move around a little to put a brake on the frenetic roundabout of his mind, for, when he was immobile, he sank slowly into his black ideas as if into shifting sands. But there was no question of going out. In the street, he had the impression that people were deliberately avoiding looking at him, as if they had all agreed to ignore him so as not to be blinded by the dazzling light of genius that radiated from him. In craven bad faith and with deadly tenacity, they were all pretending that nothing was wrong.

'Well, that's it,' he said to himself, 'I've got the *macalefu* . . .' The *macalefu* was a recipe from his home country: 'Grind up black thoughts, add two or three drops of persecution mania, a few grains of anger and a pinch of hate. Then, just simmer the whole concoction in your head.'

Once again, Joseph began pacing up and down under the inscrutable gaze of the cat, who yawned gravely.

There was only one solution.

With the shrill cry of the samurai, Joseph flung himself on Livingstone. The latter, accustomed to these surprise assaults, reacted instantly. The battle was terrible, the cat launching furious counter-attacks with his claws out and Joseph not hesitating to bite.

It was the ringing of the telephone that put an end to the bout.

83

'Yep?'

'Rapion here. Did I wake you up?'

'Er . . . no, I . . .'

'Still haven't flogged your sleep-machine, I bet?'

'Well . . .'

'I knew it. I told you so. Men are pricks, that is an eternal and metaphysical truth. Do you practise?'

'Um . . . that is, I was baptised, but . . .'

'No, I meant, do you play golf?'

'Golf? Oh, well, um . . . no.'

'Pity. Come to the golf club at Chantevaux tomorrow. I'm there every Saturday morning. It's near my factory. Let's say about eleven, if that's not too early for you. We'll talk about your lullaby-alarm.'

'Ah! . . . Are you having trouble sleeping?'

'No, but I've been thinking over what you said. In this life, one must help one's neighbour. Perhaps it's possible to help the consu . . . that is, our fellow citizens to sleep in a more active fashion . . . I mean, a little better. In any case, I'll expect you tomorrow. Goodnight!'

3

In the train that was taking him back to Paris, Joseph thought over the seductive proposition Felix Rapion had made to him. A million francs for exclusive rights to the patent, plus 10% on each machine sold. 'But what can that shark have at the back of his mind?' he wondered, smelling a rat. 'Why such an about-face? . . . *Basta*! The old vulture has realised there's money to be made and that's all there is to it.'

Joseph turned his head towards the grey suburb that was flickering past the windows. He remembered his dream of the previous autumn. 'Well,' he said to himself, 'at least there are no shit-cannons – not yet – and no advertisements in the sky.'

That evening, to celebrate his success, he made himself a giant plate of spaghetti bolognese and washed it down with a good bottle of Beaujolais. The cat was entitled to some anchovies, but he started gulping them down so voraciously that Joseph was afraid he would choke and had to take away the tin.

The meal over, Joseph sat in his dreamery and lit a cigar. Curiously enough, he felt no great elation. A weight had been taken off his back, that was all. The money he was going to earn would simply permit him not to think about money any more. There was nothing he coveted, except a few unobtainable books and an unlosable umbrella. Travel? Why, he did that every night, free of charge and with no effort. He was very proud of his contribution to the crushing of the hydra of insomnia, through his

Sleepmaker, but he could not rest on his laurels. His mind was once more off on the war-path. After conquering Italy, did not Napoleon start dreaming of Egypt?

The Sleepmaker was nothing more than an instrument of his great dream: the conquest of sleep. At the moment, it was a matter of convincing the scientific community to form a group of volunteers, a crew of hand-picked dreamers, ready to sleep come what might. He realised now that trying to set sail alone had been sheer madness. The illustrious Genoese had certainly not set off into the unknown as a lone navigator. If he had done so, even supposing he had managed to make the crossing and come back safe and sound, who would have believed in his discovery?

Joseph looked up and gazed for a long time at the portrait of his illustrious precursor, the Most Magnificent Señor Don Christopher Columbus, Grand Admiral of the Oceans, Viceroy of the Indies and discoverer of America.

At about midnight, Joseph went out. He felt more indulgent towards the human species and was in the mood for seeing people. He decided to go to the *Styx*, where Sonia worked. Perhaps he would be able to speak to her after her act. He felt in tip-top form, full of self-confidence. His success had put him back in the saddle, he felt capable of carrying off the prize.

Half an hour later, he was installed at the bar of the night club with a glass of cognac in front of him.

The place was decorated in a sort of intimate-apocalyptic style. There was an end-of-the-world atmosphere, but suitably padded. Bits of rusty iron were scattered between the tables. On the walls hung notices giving advice on survival. At the far end, there was an imitation refuse dump with the carcases of cars, stoved-in televisions and broken-down domestic appliances. The whole thing was artistically illuminated by multi-coloured spots. In the midst of the debris, a pianist dressed in rags was playing jazz on a dilapidated piano.

The waiters, dressed in anti-radiation overalls, bustled about amongst a smart and trendy clientèle.

Joseph asked the barman if it was possible to see Sonia. Yes, she always came for a drink after her number.

A few minutes later, the show began. Sonia played the part of a survivor of a nuclear holocaust. The radioactive fall-out had turned her into a nymphomaniac and she was desperately searching among the ruins for a man, but all she met with were mutants with no taste for fun and games. Suddenly, she found herself face to face with a more or less normal monkey that had escaped from a zoo. There followed a strip-tease act intended to seduce the animal. At first, the primate played hard-to-get, but finally he succumbed to the girl's charms. Hand in hand, the two of them went off to found a new human race.

It was disconcertingly amateurish and stupid enough to bring tears to the eyes. Nevertheless, the act was loudly applauded. It was true that Sonia had a superb body and her partner acted the monkey to perfection. Joseph overheard two businessmen commenting on what they had just seen.

'We don't exploit the qualities of the Frenchwoman as much as we should,' said one, 'after all, buttocks are our only raw material.'

'You're right,' agreed the other, 'if the Japanese possessed women like ours, they'd make no bones about it.'

Joseph ordered another cognac.

It was not long before Sonia appeared. She sat down beside Joseph, without seeing him, and asked for an orange juice.

'Good evening,' he said.

She turned towards him, on the defensive.

'Well, well,' she said, relaxing, 'if it isn't the sleeping doctor, come out of hibernation. Did you like my number?'

'Well . . .'

'You're right, it's dreadful. Pure nightmare. But it wasn't my idea, the owner of the night club dreamed it up . . . he's the one who plays the monkey.'

'Oh, really?

'Yes, that way he saves the expense of an actor and has a chance to get his paws on me for a while. Before, I used to do a really artistic number. I didn't try to excite men, but to disturb them . . . I made undressing mysterious. But he doesn't give a damn for art. All he wants is as many clients as possible. It's true there are more now, but just look what a bunch they are! I don't know whether they're really the avant-garde or complete pseuds, but, in any case, they're into all the latest trends. And now the boss is pestering me to make love with him on stage . . .'

'But that's revolting!' cried Joseph.

'Yes. Getting myself laid in public every night by an idiot dressed up as a monkey – no thanks! You know what I told him? I said: OK, but on condition that the monkey is a *real* one, not you!'

'And what did he say to that?'

'Oh, that he only had to snap his fingers to find girls ready to do that!'

'Why don't you look for a job somewhere else?'

'It's even worse in other places. You can't imagine the things they ask me to do.'

There was a long silence. Then Joseph, for the sake of something to say, asked, 'By the way, are the dinosaurs still stopping you from sleeping?'

'No, it's got better since I realised that it was all because of the monkey. Before that, I was trying to persuade myself that my act still had some artistic quality, that this night club was nice, that the boss had a certain charm, even as a monkey. And then I realised that I was kidding myself to make it bearable, and that, in reality, I was performing ludicrous antics in front of an audience of degenerates, and all for the sole purpose of coining money for a chimpanzee. Since I decided to call a spade a spade, I've been sleeping like a dormouse.'

The ragged pianist was once more sitting at the piano and, with the air of a zombie, tinkling out a twilight jazz tune. Joseph ordered another cognac.

'What about you?' she said, 'are you still looking for nuggets of gold in your bed?'

'Yes, but at the moment I'm not sleeping so much, I prefer to rest. This winter I perfected a Sleepmaker, a sort of anti-alarm clock. Without boasting, I believe it's an invention that will revolutionise the history of sleep.'

'And you're making this thing yourself?'

'No, I've been offered a contract by an industrialist, a contract that could earn me a great deal of money.'

She pulled a face, as if disillusioned and said, 'I see you haven't entirely renounced the goodies of this world, then.'

'Oh! But I'm not sure yet if I'm going to sign,' said Joseph though he was perfectly sure he would. 'Certainly,' he added, 'I'm a little uneasy at the idea of entrusting my machine to a vulgar manufacturer of chemical turds, but I didn't invent this apparatus just to put it in my cellar and lull the rats to sleep. Besides, the distribution of my Sleepmaker will earn me a certain fame, and that will allow me to fulfil my project for the conquest of sleep. It will all turn out fine in the end – my future and the future of the world! My mission is to sleep with all my strength, my duty is to dream come hell or high water. I am convinced that man's future lies in sleep, and the keys to that future are to be found in our beds, and in mine in particular. I have a solemn responsibility towards mankind, and I won't shirk it. Next summer, there'll be a conference on sleep in Tahiti. I shall deliver a historic speech there. I will persuade the scientific community to organise a crew to set sail for the isles of sleep.'

'Oh! So now there are islands?'

'Yes,' replied Joseph fervently, 'there are islands, an archipelago of dreams where, thanks to my vessel of sleep – my sleep machine – I will land as a conqueror in the name of humanity! In the early days, we shall have to be careful of shifting sands, unknown creatures, mysterious plants. Some valiant sleepers

89

will perish. But, little by little, we shall gain confidence, learn to avoid the pitfalls of sleep, then we'll begin to extract its riches, to exploit the mines of knowledge and poetry, and we will bring back from down there the fruits of knowledge as the conquistadores of Peru brought back gold.'

'You're a dreamer full of will and ambition.'

'I aspire to glory, I won't deny that. But I won't commit the mistake Christopher Columbus made, I won't demand the title of Grandee of Spain and Viceroy of the Indies. One must be a realist. The eternal gratitude of mankind will be enough for me.'

'And besides, if you were appointed Viceroy of the Indies, you'd be obliged to go there from time to time, and it's hot . . . that's not good for the brain.'

'Yes . . . Oh, by the way, I was thinking . . . um . . . what would you say to coming to Tahiti with me? It would get you out of this rat-hole. I'd try not to make a nuisance of myself. I may not seem very cheerful at the moment, but that's because, for too long now, worry has been my pillow and solitude my blanket. And . . . and because I never know when I should keep my mouth shut nor how to talk without actually saying anything. Moreover, I often get irritable, for not only do I love truth, but also, for my pains, I hate lies, falsity and bad faith. But, except that I don't talk much, never smile and often get ratty, I don't think I'm a disagreeable companion.'

'To tell you the truth, I don't know if I'm worthy to travel with a genius.'

'Genius, genius! Let's not exaggerate – although I certainly don't reject the title *a priori*. But, even if the word could legitimately be applied to myself, I must point out that it is the virtue of a genius not to elevate himself above others, but rather to penetrate into the soul of each man. And, like the sun, genius illumines everybody.'

'I admit I'm a little afraid of getting sunstroke. Anyway, I'll think over your offer. Or rather, I'll dream about it.'

'Yes, have happy dreams about it because – '

Joseph was interrupted by a series of muffled explosions that shook the room and made the glasses rattle.

'What's that?' he exclaimed.

'Don't be alarmed,' said Sonia, 'the boss has installed a machine that makes imitation air raids. It's effective, huh?'

'Yes,' Joseph replied, 'totally idiotic, but effective.'

Under the fictitious bombardment, the regular customers brightened up. The electricity was cut off, candles were lit. Waiters wearing gas-masks served champagne.

4

A few days later, Joseph signed the contract and handed the prototype of his Sleepmaker over to Rapion.

From that moment, Joseph was a rich man. He wandered round Paris like a lost soul, looking for something to buy.

He came home with his arms full of parcels. He bought himself: a pair of silk pyjamas decorated with gold braid (when he saw his reflection in the mirror, he thought he looked ridiculous); an umbrella with a cord that could be attached to the wrist (but it was red with green dots); a futuristic pen that filled electronically with special ink for writing under water (he dared not use it for fear of breaking it). For Livingstone, he bought a collar with a little golden bell on it and some lamb's brains. The cat approved of and ate the brains, but there was no way he was going to let Joseph try the collar on him.

In the long run, the only purchase that really gave Joseph any pleasure was an old edition of the *Fables* of La Fontaine illustrated by Grandville, and it cost him only a few francs at a bookstall.

He realised with a shock that it was not in the least necessary to possess a fortune to acquire the things he loved best in all the world, namely: books and spaghetti. True, there were women, but . . . it was something he just couldn't help, he *could* not take any interest in mercenary women.

Moreover, he soon became aware that he was not all that rich. For the first time in his life, he experienced a sense of material deprivation, money having placed him in situations in which he needed still more of the stuff. For example, he planned to buy a flat and, throughout an exhausting week, searched for one that would suit him. And all the ones he liked turned out to be beyond his means. In effect, he had simply passed from the status of a relatively rich man amongst the poor to that of a poor man amongst the rich.

But there was worse. As if under some evil spell, Joseph's small fortune made him hanker after precisely those things that were not for sale. He was obssessed by Sonia. He started looking at himself in the mirror and counting his white hairs. He worried so much about his health that it brought on headaches. Then he remembered a parable he had heard in his childhood, and the way an old man in his village, sitting by his hearth with chestnuts sizzling and popping in front of him, had related it: 'If you want to gather wild asparagus in the woods, there are two places you can go . . . you can go down into the valley, but afterwards you will have to climb up again. You can climb higher up the mountain, above the village, but afterwards you will have to come down again. What you gain now, you will lose later. Time breaks everything and Time repairs everything. The man who has everything watches the fleeting years with anxiety, the man who has been battered by life looks with tenderness upon nature, upon the earth where he will soon lie. The one is wretched in his happiness, the other is happy in his wretchedness.'

With a Havana in his mouth, Joseph surveyed his dreamery and thought: 'The fellow who takes the metro every day dreams of his approaching holidays, which are not too far away. But the man who has everything and rides round in a Rolls Royce . . . what can he dream of? Of immortality, which he can never attain . . . but that doesn't stop me preferring a Rolls to the metro.'

As glory began to loom up on the horizon, Joseph's congenital melancholy was transformed into exasperated impatience. His despair which, after all, had been quite peaceful and even cosy to live with, had given way to anguished waiting. Marking time on the threshold of Paradise is worse than roasting in hell. When the gates of Celebrity open, hope no longer gives you a moment's repose, it keeps you simmering over a low flame, it hangs on to your coat-tails and kicks you up the backside all the time. Joseph could no longer bear the fact that he, the inventor of the Sleepmaker, the genius of sleep, was still standing in the shadows, as lonely as a dead rat. Consciousness of his superiority tormented him. It seemed an abominable injustice that nobody recognised him in the street. 'Patience, patience!' he muttered, watching the people who were crammed on to the terraces of the cafés in these first fine days of May. 'Soon, they'll be fighting to get near me!'

But, in the meantime, he was nothing but a poor caterpillar in a hurry to become a butterfly, even if the metamorphosis would inevitably attract the collector's net. And Joseph, who at one time would have consoled himself with some beautiful thought, now tried to raise his spirits by looking for something to buy.

In the early evenings, he went to the *Amis du Sport* for an apéritif. One day, he could no longer contain himself. After paying for a round of drinks, as a means of preparing the ground, he hinted tactfully that he was a genius but, for technical reasons, would prefer to remain in the shadow just for the present. Thanks to him, science was about to take a giant step forward, he could say no more than that.

The *belote*-players listened to him politely. The Father of the People, no doubt embittered by the incident with the coffee-machine, started suddenly at the word 'science' and declared in an icy tone, 'Science, monsieur, is boiled beef for cats. They know how to cultivate bacteria all right, but they no longer know how to bring up kids. They can juggle with atoms, but courtesy has been forgotten. They travel in space but the sea stinks and the fish are dying. They spend more money on rockets than on food for people dying of starvation. The truth is, the more they know about things, the less they know how to live. If the only purpose of science is to brain-wash whole nations and transform the planet into an anthill with all mod. cons., no thanks, says I! I'd prefer to hunt lions and whoop it up every night, like the Papuans. Technology doesn't make men better, it just makes evil ten times more powerful. The same halfwit who, ten thousand years ago, used to chuck stones at the birds when he blew his top, can nowadays shoot a missile at a 'plane full of people. Progress doesn't diminish human stupidity, it simply makes it more dangerous.'

During the days and nights that followed, these remarks obsessed Joseph. When it came right down to it, what was his research into sleep worth, when you considered all the distress in the world? Entire nations reduced to poverty by the financial manoeuvring of a handful of vampires; whole cultures wiped out or whittled into folklore for tourists; everywhere love was giving way to an anguished quest for pleasure; literature was degraded to the role of a mere accomplishment, like a flower glued on a bulldozer; nature was systematically being plundered to squeeze out the maximum profit . . . it was as if man were sawing through the branch he was sitting on. Certainly, it would take more than a sleep machine to awaken mankind from its nightmare . . .

It was about this time that he began to dream of the Grand Inquisitor.

5

One day, when Joseph flew into the *Amis du Sport* with his cat by his side, The Father of the People announced serenely that a man dressed in black had come in and demanded his death. 'If I were you,' added the Father of the People, 'I'd pack my traps and go and look for myself somewhere else.' Joseph, incapable of rising into the air again, walked out of the café and woke up with stomach cramps from fear.

The Grand Inquisitor was looking for him. Sleep is vast, tortuous and immensely deep, but the Grand Inquisitor had all the time in the world. The Grand Inquisitor, in fact, was no longer dependent on time.

From that moment, Joseph was a hunted sleeper. He avoided lingering in his dreams. When a nightmare went on too long, he took any train whatever, insisting on a ticket that would not take him anywhere. Or he got into a bus whose destination he did not know and got off at some forgotten bus-stop, lost in the depths of the night. But still he felt the haunting presence of his pursuer, just a few ravelled skeins of sleep behind him.

Every time he went to bed now, he was in a state of anguish. In a bed, all things are possible. There is nothing to prevent the worst. Sleep is a blank page on which anything whatsoever can be written. Joseph tried sleeping diagonally, with one foot on the floor, to avoid being sucked down into a nightmare and becoming a prey to the horrors.

One night, he found himself in front of a vast cathedral. There was a menu pinned to the door and, as he felt hungry, he went in.

The interior was like an immense classroom with the individual dining-tables facing the altar. Gentlemen wearing white shirts, ties, jackets and shorts were piously eating as they followed the service. A priestess who resembled Sonia was doing a religious strip-tease. Joseph sat down discreetly at a table. Choirboys brought him a plate of spaghetti and a bottle of wine. The priestess, displaying her buttocks to the rapt congregation, intoned, 'This is my arse . . .', then, with a cold eye that contrasted with her warm loins, she started panting, as if she were making love with some invisible entity, perhaps with God. Just then, there was a loud knocking on the cathedral doors. In a moment, there was total uproar. 'The Grand Inquisitor!' shouted the people, seized with panic. Joseph, sweating with anxiety, managed to escape through a crypt that debouched into a metro station.

From that night on, he had a fear of closed doors, even when awake.

He knew he was risking his neck. The ancient authors record numerous examples of fatality during sleep, and he personally had known of several cases of nocturnal decease due to heart attacks brought on by nightmares. He even remembered one patient who had laughed himself to death during his siesta. Fear or joy, pleasure or nostalgia, love or hate, all the emotions are intensified by sleep since reason no longer intervenes to curb them. It can also happen that the heart simply gives out: the dreamer is not always equal to his dream. Moreover, we dream not only out of our individual experience as domesticated and civilised citizens, with a set routine and a clearly-defined life-style, but also out of the experience of our species, acquired over millions of years. The sensations felt by a Neanderthal man faced with a mammoth can surge up again in the sleeping brain of a Parisian. But the image in his dream will not be that of a mammoth. It might be, for instance, his boss, or a cop with a riot shield snarling at him.

And so, the safety of the bed is illusory. Certainly, under the duvet covers, you run no risk of being devoured by a giant spider, but you can be devoured by your own terror. And Joseph was terrified. Not of dying, for, in his dreams, he was often dead. It was not that he was afraid of anything in particular, he was afraid, and that was all. It was as if he had a mouth inside his stomach, a mouth that would suddenly and without warning gnaw at his entrails, whether he was asleep or awake, lying down or standing up. If a crocodile had come slithering into his dreamery, it would have produced little effect on him, in fact, he would probably – no, certainly – have given it a big welcome, for a crocodile is solid, reliable, you know what you're dealing with. But that meta-physical gobbledygook that seized hold of him out of the blue, when he least expected it, while he was cooking his spaghetti or lacing up his shoes . . . what could he do about that? Nothing, because this blue funk was, by definition, nothing. Nothing in all its horror. The nothing that leaps at our throats to remind us that we ourselves are nothing.

No, there is nothing you can do against nothing.

And this nothing is always worse in bed. Awake, Joseph could withstand it better, he could move around, walk in circles, or in zigzags, doing a zig when the nothing was doing a zag and a zag when the nothing was doing a zig. But . . . his dreams were beginning to seep out under the door of sleep. Corridors, stairways, street-corners, everything he saw reminded him of some nightmare or other. His entire existence was stamped with the seal of horror. The walls of sleep were cracking and the anguish of his nights was oozing out through all the cracks and insinuating itself into his daily life. Like Ch'uan-tsao-she who, having dreamed of being a butterfly, wondered whether he were not really a butterfly dreaming of being Ch'uan-tsao-she, Joseph began to have doubts about the nature of the waking man. He felt much more real once he was asleep. Insomniacs have trouble finding sleep, but Joseph had trouble finding the waking state. In his dreams, he had to deal with concrete things, things with their own tenacious existence, things with a tried and tested reality.

Awake, he felt he was in a cloud. A cloud where the only concrete thing was anxiety.

Sleeping or waking, for Joseph it was simply a change of fear. Awake, fear meant suddenly having cotton-wool knees, an octopus where his stomach ought to be, not knowing which end of things to get hold of, the anguish of having two eyes, a nose and a mouth . . . Asleep, fear was absolutely anything. When you're asleep, you don't need monsters, you can be reduced to jelly by a wine-funnel, a Basque beret, a bicycle. For in the profound depths of sleep, the world no longer presents itself to your view, it leaps out at you. Things are no longer seen in terms of their function, but become what they are, in all their splendour and abomination.

Every evening, Joseph disconnected the telephone, put on his battle pyjamas, glanced under the bed, turned over his bolster and slipped between the sheets, ready to attack the night. Knowing that he was about to go into combat, he might have been inclined to delay his bedtime, but he preferred to go to bed fighting fit. His sleep was full of perilous rocks; to set sail amongst them weakened by fatigue would have been reckless to the point of folly.

In the darkness, Joseph did mental arithmetic to calm his anxiety and induce sleep. (Numbers had always had a soporific effect on him. At high school, he often used to fall asleep during the mathematics lessons.) Figures lulled him. Little by little, they began to interact with one another, they sucked each other in, penetrated and impregnated each other, went limp, dilated again, bit their tails, rolled up into wheels, metamorphosed at random. Unheard-of figures sprang out of the dark, supraterrestrial numbers that suddenly split in two and disgorged millions of bizarrely-shaped insects . . .

Each morning, on waking, it was as if he had reached port after enduring a stormy night at the helm of his bed. Clinging to his pillow, a haggard survivor of the maelstrom of sleep, he made his entry into the roadsteads of reality. He wiped the sweat off his face with a handkerchief, got up feebly, pushed his feet into his slippers, looked with bleary eyes at the bed rumpled by his tumultuous crossing, and mechanically followed the cat, who guided him to the fridge. Once more, he had escaped the dreaded Inquisitor. But for how long? At present, he was an outlaw of sleep, a panic-stricken runaway who hugged the walls, kept away from doorways, avoided loitering in the streets and averted his eyes from things for fear they would turn into something loathsome. He slept like a fugitive. Every night, the city of sleep became more oppressive. It was a ghetto, he could only move around clandestinely, the streets were blocked by brick walls, grass grew between the tramlines, there were forbidden tunnels, cul-de-sacs, barred windows, stopped clocks, split plane-trees and a station where the feverish passengers whispered into each other's ears the mysterious timetables of hypothetical trains.

One morning, as he was watching the comings and goings of the men delivering vegetables in the street below, Joseph was struck by a sudden revelation. He cried out, 'If I don't move my arse, I'm done for!'

What he lacked was action, exercise! That was what his dreams were trying to tell him! Stagnating in his flat, moving neither hand nor foot, he had fallen into himself as into a bottomless well. Life is dynamic, things can only be weighed correctly when in motion. His ideas were paralysing him, his imagination always ran on ahead of events and convinced him of the disappointing end-results of all action before he had even begun to do whatever it was: if he thought of picking a flower, he imagined it already withered. But, if he continued to do nothing, he would come to a sticky end. Still water stagnates. Moving would make him lighter, it would give him back his taste for life! A pleasant voyage, that would purge his head!

What if he indulged in a little cruise, now he had the means?

Yes, that was an excellent idea. In this way, while travelling in comfort, he could avoid all those visits to museums, there would be no monuments to gape at, he could rest in the shade and save himself the trouble of tramping the streets in search of a decent restaurant. The ocean, nothing but the ocean! At least the sea is solid! He would choose a cruise in the Pacific so as to be on the spot for the conference on sleep in Tahiti. He would prepare his epoch-making speech on board ship. Perhaps Sonia would agree to come with him. That would be marvellous!

Ah! To set sail, to cast off one's moorings! A change of atmosphere, a change of beds . . . why on earth hadn't he thought of it before? And who knows? Perhaps this way he could shake off the Grand Inquisitor . . .

6

14 June. A calm night. I dreamed I was lying in a bed with a sail, floating on a transparent ocean. Millions of multicoloured fish and the most extraordinary creatures appeared under my bed, right down into the unsoundable depths.

Tomorrow I'm flying to Marseilles and, the same evening, I shall embark on the *Akhenaton*, which will drop anchor in Papeete on 15 August, the opening day of the conference on sleep. Livingstone is boarding with The Father of the People, who has a small garden and three large cats. Livingstone intensely dislikes the company of his brothers, but I think it will do him good. Living alone, he is acquiring as many fads as an old bachelor. He's becoming a little boorish and only purrs once in a blue moon.

I rang Sonia. A cruise is out of the question, she's afraid of sea-sickness. She's still hesitating about Tahiti. I'll send her a plane ticket, she can do what she likes with it. She's beginning to get on my nerves. She doesn't know what she wants. Or rather, she knows only too well. In her search for a made-to-measure man, she will find nothing but a robot. *Basta*! I've decided not to think about her any more. And the best way to stop thinking about a woman is to start thinking about another woman. On the boat, I am sure to find one I can dream about in peace.

17 June. Magnificent cruise. This immaculate white boat is very spacious, thus allowing me to avoid overcrowding. My cabin is

102

pleasant and my bed works well. I take my meals alone, looking out over the sea. On deck, I have a corner to myself with a little table where I am writing these lines. There's a cup of coffee beside me. I have started drafting my Tahitian lecture, which will be entitled: *Prelude to the Conquest of the Empire of Sleep*. I can assert, here and now, that this text will be a milestone in the history of human thought. For the moment, only the sun and the sea understand me. I am trying to resist the contempt I feel for all these half-witted passengers who do not recognise my greatness and know nothing of the mission with which Providence has entrusted me. Well, chin up! Their indifference will be just one more leaf in my laurel wreath!

Not a sign of the Grand Inquisitor on the horizon.

19 June. After several days at sea, the passengers are beginning to get bored stiff in spite of the cretinous games with which they are spoon-fed. I pity them because they are not used to doing nothing. As soon as they stop dashing about, they're like invalids. Some of them sit in deck-chairs doing crosswords and soaking up the sun, determined to get a good tan or die. Others, bewildered by inactivity, trail pathetically around the deck looking for something to photograph, like dogs looking for a bone. Still others spend their time foraging in the shops on board, where you can find all sorts of useless gadgets and luxurious knick-knacks at exorbitant prices. Obviously, they're all sick. The hyperactivity of modern life has atrophied their ability to contemplate and, if I can express it like this, their muscle of idleness. They have forgotten how to do nothing. Left to themselves, they're like hens who have hatched out a duckling. Their only mental occupation is persuading themselves they are happy.

*

21 June. Glorious sleep. I dreamed with great panache, accomplishing exploits which, alas! I cannot remember.

Off the coast of Mauretania, some poverty-stricken fishermen came aboard to try and sell traditional souvenirs and trinkets. The passengers were delighted – at last, something new to buy!

22 June. I dreamed this sentence: The best thing I have is that which I lack.

23 June. The chaise-longue is man's noblest achievement. The white flight of the seagulls wipes out my black thoughts, the sea rocks me gently. O wild sea, full of treasures and nightmares, of marvels and horrors, you are brute reality, the very opposite of mind! In you, reason is drowned, you are incomprehensible because you understand everything, you are made of the stuff of dreams!

25 June. I dreamed a definition of immobility: IMMOBILITY IS THAT WHICH IS SLOWER THAN SLOW AND TRAVELS FASTER THAN SPEED.

I also dreamed that, in the language of sleep, the moon is called *Yol* and the sun *Sarabraxas*. I have started compiling a French–Sleep glossary.

27 June. He's back. O God, it was horrible! I still did not see him but I could feel him so close to me! I was at the end of a deserted avenue, bordered with plane-trees, which rose up steeply in front of me. At the top of the hill, there was a bed standing vertically on end, and on it, with his hands and feet nailed to the sheets, was a crucified monk. It was the Spanish monk, the one who escaped through sleep from the dungeons of the Holy Office! The Grand Inquisitor must eventually have caught up with him!

I woke up in a pool of sweat, my heart palpitating. It took me ten minutes to screw up the courage to move.

It was all very well telling myself I was a prey to my own imagination, it did not reassure me in the least for, in my head, there are things a thousand times worse than anything in reality, and those very things might be the death of me.

I have tried to master the world of ideas, yet here I am, the plaything of my anxieties. I, who lay claim to the throne of sleep, am hounded by a nightmare!

28 June. He has left me in peace, but still I go to sleep in a state of Angst, not knowing where I shall land up.

Solitude is dragging me down into the deepest parts of my interior being. I have actually made a few attempts to get to know some of the passengers, but formulating banal phrases and behaving as if nothing was the matter has become a form of torture. By the time I have thought up something to say, the conversation has moved to another subject. How quickly platitudes pass! I think I would feel more at ease faced with a rhinoceros than with a Chief Accountant on holiday.

The only person I managed to chat with never let me get a word in edgeways: a writer suffering from exhaustion and a paucity of inspiration. It was his publisher who sent him off on this cruise. He told me how many copies of his books have been printed and the prizes they have won, talked about the ministers he knows intimately and the translation of his novels into Serbo-Croat and Javanese. 'I said this, I did that, I know So-and-so, I sold so many . . .' and this went on for two hours. By gargling all these words, he tries to forget the void within him and the nothingness that awaits him.

29 June. In a dream, I received a letter from the Grand Inquisitor. He advised me to take stock of myself. There were some words I did not understand, and they froze my blood. He called me a *Callouskin*, the worst insult in the language of sleep.

The fish don't know how happy they are . . . which is the chief condition for being happy.

30 June. No significant dreams. The Grand Inquisitor must be sharpening up his weapons.

The moment I lie down, I start reviewing my life. I am afraid of all the things that might happen, and still more afraid that nothing will happen.

The writer spends his time gazing at the sea like an idiot and searching for ideas. I spoke to him again, or rather, we spoke about him. I get the impression he writes books, not out of a love for life, but out of a disgust for everything. He makes money out of his disgust. The only thing that interests him, apart from himself, is stuffing his guts. What strange times we live in, when cheese-makers chat about Proust and writers discourse on camembert!

3 July. I have a feeling the Grand Inquisitor is cooking something up. He is waiting for a propitious moment, like a tiger lying in wait. To die during a nightmare must be appalling, for sleep amplifies everything and time seems endless. I put a terrifying question to myself. Could the Grand Inquisitor incarcerate me for ever in a dream, shut me up for all eternity in a dungeon of sleep?

6 July. Calm sea, blue sky. First cases of depression on board. More and more I pity these people who embarked so light-heartedly, without any experience of idleness. I see them trailing round the deck, crushed by boredom. If you're not used to doing nothing, you shouldn't go on a cruise, for Christ's sake! Unlike the common hustle and bustle, which is within everybody's reach, *farniente*, doing nothing, is a difficult art, not to be attained by amateurs. I myself still have a long way to go, for, while doing nothing is easy for me, the real problem is to *think* nothing.

This afternoon, off the coast of Madagascar, we saw shark fins cutting through the water. A few minutes later, we heard a great '*plop*!' It was the writer, who had just thrown himself into the sea. Everybody rushed to the rails to watch the spectacle. The children clapped, the women let out little 'oohs' and 'ahs' of excitement, the men frantically reloaded their cameras. Near me, a fat female with two rows of pearls and three rows of chins yelped at her husband, 'Albert! Albert! Come quickly and see, they're going to eat him!'

But the sharks were finicky. The flesh of a successful writer must be a little too fatty for them. Someone threw him a lifebelt. He hung on to it but refused categorically to be hauled back on board. He kept braying: 'I'm worthless! I'm worthless! Let me sink!' The Captain tried to reason with him, but he kept playing the prima donna, bobbing about in the waves. In the end, out of lassitude or boredom, the sharks started swimming towards him. Monsieur then graciously consented to being hauled up.

Restless nights. I dream that I cannot get to sleep, or that I cannot wake up.

9 July. I have seen the door! I almost opened it! It was the door that leads to coma, to the sleep from which there is no awaking! It is a white door with a round brass handle. It stands at the end of a cul-de-sac. Behind it is a garden, the garden of eternal sleep. If I had opened that door, I would have been a prisoner of sleep for ever, at the mercy of the Grand Inquisitor. It was Livingstone who saved me. He climbed on to my umbrella and miaouwed into my ear that he didn't like sardine-tails, which was code for 'You mustn't open that door!' I escaped by the skin of my teeth!

*

10 July. The sun is shining, the sky is blue, but I am still thinking too much. My internal cinema-show projects itself onto the ocean, and it's always the same films that run and rerun, sinister films in which I play the most wretched role. My past makes me choke and the vision of my future ties my bowels in knots.

I have made it a rule not to reflect in the abstract, never to think of things I can do nothing about and to keep my imagination on a tight rein. Illusion and revulsion are two sides of the same coin. Castles in Spain are steeped in gloom.

My lecture is coming on fine. When I write, things miraculously make sense. I have doubts about the universe but am sure of my sentences. The sea inspires me. It is gentle, terrible and mysterious, like dreams, immense, profound and fertile, like sleep.

12 July. I was running like the devil down a road with the Grand Inquisitor on my heels. He was armed with a saw and I could hear him panting behind me. At the last moment, I managed to fly away. I am sick of being afraid.

The writer is holed up in his cabin. They say he has started writing a new book, about his experience with the sharks. I made a final attempt to speak to someone. He was a good-natured fellow who introduced himself as the King of the Nappy-de-luxe. For an hour, he chatted to me about his dogs. The Nappy King and the Emperor of Sleep discussing the psychology of poodles in the middle of the Indian Ocean – what a perfect nightmare!

15 July. Last night, everybody stuffed themselves to the gills and then we had fireworks and a grand ball. False jollity, fixed grins, stupidity triumphant. How is it that people don't realise a genuine sadness is more stimulating than a fictitious gaiety? If they really let themselves go, they would fall on their knees and weep. I hate festivities. I walked up and down the deck, gazing at the stars.

108

Decidedly, I felt closer to the constellations than to those bloated bipeds obsessed with the idea of enjoying themselves to the hilt and squeezing the maximum profit out of everything that comes their way. I think that, for those who have twisted minds, pleasure itself becomes poison, just as glory becomes a burden to those who do not deserve it.

The faint lights of a fishermen's village, which I saw glimmering on a little island in the distance, give me back a little faith in mankind. In my cabin, I worked on my Tahitian speech to the rhythm of the water lapping against the hull.

17 July. I dreamed that Sonia and the Grand Inquisitor were making love. I've had enough of this crazy fanatic who is the holy terror of sleep! I long to set an ambush for him at the corner of a dream and catch him by the coat-tails! We will settle our accounts with our bare fists, as between sleepers!

19 July. We called in at Madras. I didn't go ashore, the city looked like an anthill on the point of collapse.

I bought a prayer-wheel from a native who came on board. It is a marvellous device for making one think less. The rhythm of the cylinder and the incessant movement of the hand have the virtue of chasing away doubt and cleansing the mind.

The more you seek for sleep, the more it eludes you. By the same token, the more you ask yourself questions, the further you are from finding the answers. As the underground root nourishes the tree, so the things we are unaware of nourish our lives. Once the scientists reach a perfect understanding of what sleep is, the entire world will be a prey to insomnia. When we become masters of all things, we will have become purely mechanical consuming machines, devoid of all faith in life. Anguished puppets manipulated by abstractions.

*

21 July. Ghastly nightmare. I was coming out of a hospital belonging to the Holy Office and I was no longer whole. I walked through Paris knowing some part of my body was missing, but not knowing which it was. I no longer dared look at myself in a mirror. When they saw me, passers-by took off their hats and crossed themselves.

24 July. In the ghetto of sleep, where I am on the run throughout my feverish nights, I have glimpsed other fugitive dreamers. We were not able to communicate, but understood tacitly that it is dangerous to use certain words or to call things by their proper name. The walls have ears and the doors have eyes. You are so frightened that you are even afraid to show fear, for it might bring a punishment down on your head. Prudence dictates, therefore, that you should never say what you think and always keep a contented expression on your face. Is truth always clandestine?

27 July. Port of call at Darwin, Australia. I went ashore for a few hours intending to see some kangaroos. I am very interested in their means of locomotion, their great parabolic leaps, which I myself can use at will during my dreams (even more than actual flight). I think there must be some connection between jumping and sleeping, especially as kangaroos are reputed to be great sleepers. I would not be surprised if sleep-walking is a particularly important activity among them, nor that their specific way of leaping, typical of their species, has been developed thanks to an intensive practice of sleep. So, I disembarked, but oh! what a disappointment! No more kangaroos in Darwin than there are fishbones in a turkey. The aborigines could not supply me with one. Here, the animal is considered to be too common to put in a zoo and too cumbersome to keep as a pet. In reply to my repeated questions, they pointed evasively to the outback. It did not take me long to work out that, in Australia, kangaroos are

110

really frowned upon (which, to be honest, confirms them in my good opinion). They are accused of being intrusive, stupid and inedible. That's exactly what I think about men. Coming back on board, I felt ashamed of a humanity that can ignore this marvellous leaping animal, this high-flying sleeper, to whom all civilisations worthy of the name should devote a cult.

30 July. I am wandering through dim-lit streets, like a conspirator hunted by the Sleep Police. I am searching for the only people who could save me, but I have lost their address. Sometimes, at the corner of a dark alley, or in a half-opened doorway, I believe I see the phantom of a woman I once loved.

3 August. Ordinary nightmares. My Tahitian lecture is progressing admirably. In the mornings, I sit on deck in my pyjamas and work on it. As I hone my phrases, I spin the prayer-wheel to chase away irrelevant thoughts. Sometimes I exchange a glance with some women passengers, who are watching me from the upper deck and giving me significant looks. Thanks to their feminine intuition they undoubtedly sense that they are in the presence of an exceptional man.

6 August. Clammy nightmares, fugitive nights.

I am not thinking so much about Sonia. Having dreamed of her so often, I begin to be weary of her. He who sleeps, dines. Nevertheless, I have sent her a 'plane ticket for Tahiti.

10 August. For the first time, I have heard the Grand Inquisitor's voice. I bolted through a door in nameless terror and heard him shout, 'When I've finished with you, you'll be as flat as a Breton crêpe!'

111

12 August. The Grand Inquisitor is on my heels. I am afraid, but I believe he is, too. I represent a terrible threat to his authority. He knows the nature of my ambitions. He will do anything to prevent my establishing my sovereignty over the empire of sleep. But I have finished my lecture and I will deliver it, come hell or high water.

In my position, anybody else would be seized with delusions of grandeur, but I am keeping a cool head. I will demand nothing – neither titles nor medals nor money. I will be content with Glory. I am too great a soul to sink into megalomania.

7

It was a mere shadow of a man who disembarked at Papeete. He was thinner, his face was like *papier mâché*, his eyes glittered with exaltation and sadness. There emanated from him an indefinable air of distress and a brooding silence. After an overworked *vahina* with a regulation smile on her face had placed the traditional necklace of flowers around his neck, Joseph settled into the Hôtel de l'Avenir et du Commerce Réunis.

He arranged his belongings in his room, took off the garland, hid his lecture under the mattress (solitude had made him distrustful) and went out again with his umbrella for company.

He liked the feel of an umbrella in his hand. It reassured him, gave him a hold on reality. It was like a hyphen between himself and the world. Even in dreams, the umbrella rarely left him and had more than once saved the situation. In the hands of an experienced dreamer, an umbrella can be a redoubtable weapon and a most convenient means of locomotion.

Joseph had to cross the town to get to the Palais des Congrès. Several times he was almost run over, for he had not imagined there would be cars in Tahiti.

Papeete, in fact, is simply palm trees with vehicles all around them. Or, to be more precise, vehicles with some palm trees in their midst. And Joseph saw the same things one sees in every city: dog-shit, plastic bags, traffic lights, telephone kiosks, estate agents, supermarkets and apathetic people. True, there were some beautiful *vahinas*, but they were all too busy playing the part of beautiful *vahinas*.

Like flies round a jam-jar, the tourists were swarming in all directions, disdainful of one another, anxious to relax, hunting for souvenirs the moment they set foot on the island, automatically photographing everything that looked Tahitian and eyeing the prices suspiciously, determined to get the best out of everything and not miss a trick.

It was distressing. Tahiti was like an old whore, outrageously made-up and covered with ants.

When Joseph reached the Palais des Congrès, the inaugural cocktail party was in full swing. He recognised several big cheeses in the field of sleep, having seen their photographs in scientific magazines. Notably, the famous Professor Mac Philox, specialist in tsetse flies, the illustrious Zuyong Hua, the high priest of yawning, Professor Denis de Haultequeue, author of a magisterial thesis on the sleep of the orang-utan, and the celebrated Wilhelm von Schnopf, who had dedicated his life to somnambulism in tortoises. Felix Rapion, the discreet organiser of the conference, was taking no part in it.

Joseph, being neither the type who haunts conferences, nor a scribbler of articles, did not know a soul. He accepted a martini from a half-naked *vahina* and, yawning, observed the top brass of sleep. With great animation, they were discussing theories about falling asleep and, at the same time, eyeing the long-dreamed-of *vahinas* who were serving the drinks.

'If they only knew what I've got in store for them . . .' he mused.

Meanwhile, he noticed that chilling looks were being turned furtively in his direction. He thought he heard his name mentioned, and those little smiles of contempt . . . what did they signify? Perhaps they were all in the know already about his invention and the forthcoming marketing of his Sleepmaker, but why this hostility? Was it jealousy? Joseph made an attempt to join in one or other of the discussions but, as soon as he approached a group, backs were turned and everyone avoided his eye.

Suddenly, he felt some menace at his back.

Small-time dreamers are inclined to turn away from danger, to run away at the least sign of peril. It is only élite sleepers who know that the monster will only grow larger if you don't look it in the eye, and that, in all circumstances, awake or dreaming, it is best to follow the immortal advice of the air ace Guynemer: *Face up to it*. Joseph therefore turned round briskly, his jaws clenched, his hand tightening on his umbrella. He found himself nose to nose with a fellow who was grinning from ear to ear.

Joseph had only seen him once before in his life, but he knew him well because he had dreamed about him several times, and these dreams had been more like nightmares. He was a young, aggressively ambitious doctor by the name of Binard with whom Joseph had had dealings when his Sleepmaker was being tested at the Salpêtrière Hospital. At that time, this phoney little bull-shitter had shown him utter indifference, but now he seemed delighted at rediscovering him in Tahiti. His face expressed boundless admiration, approaching ecstasy.

'You remember me, don't you, Dr Cavalcanti?' he said in honeyed tones, his mouth pursed up like a hen's arse.

'Yes,' replied Joseph coldly, 'I remember you very well.'

'What do you think of Tahiti? Marvellous, isn't it? Extraordinary! The sky, the sea, these lovely simple people . . .'

'To tell you the truth, I have dreamed it better. The Tahiti of my dreams was more like the real thing. More authentic. More Tahitian, in fact.'

Frowning, Binard shook his head gravely to show that he was aware of the profundity of Joseph's words, and answered obsequiously, 'Our dreams are always far more beautiful than the pale reality . . .'

"The only advantage of reality is that it is real.'

'Ah, yes, indeed, reality is real,' Binard agreed dreamily.

'By the way, Dr Binard, perhaps it's my imagination, but I get the feeling the gentlemen at this conference are giving me the cold shoulder.'

115

'Oh, that's certainly on account of your machine. There have been some leaks. Now everybody knows all about Monsieur Rapion's plans. What can you expect, innovations always provoke criticism from those who are against progress and are condemned outright by the narrow-minded. Even the inventor of the zip fastener had to face the incomprehension of his contemporaries, yet where would we be today without zip fasteners? One zip and, hey presto! I myself am in favour of everything that is new, on principle. Novelty is the future.'

'But my apparatus isn't justifiable solely on the grounds that it's new – '

'You're right, it must also be profitable.'

'No, I wasn't thinking of that, I was going to say that my Sleepmaker is also useful, it can be beneficial to people . . .'

Raising his voice now, so as to be heard by the members of the conference, who were sipping their cocktails and chatting, Joseph went on, 'The sleep it induces is a healthy sleep, a real sleep, unlike that induced by sleeping pills, which disrupt the whole organism, stifle the natural oneiric activity and transform people into larvae! But the gentlemen who specialise in sleep never breathe a word about the damage caused by sleeping pills, or, at most, only in whispers, so as not to offend those poisoners of the population who give rewards to those who know how to keep their mouths shut!'

A silence had fallen, and all those present were looking at Joseph with an embarrassed air. Binard, misinterpreting Joseph's reaction, said softly, to calm him, 'Personally, I'm convinced your machine will sell well and bring you plenty of money.'

Then with a perfectly odious conspiratorial wink, he added in a whisper, 'Your sleep-machine is a little gold-mine!'

'A gold-mine!' roared Joseph, so loudly that all the members of the conference and all the *vahinas* jumped, 'A gold-mine! Do you think I've been killing myself, dreaming for years and years without a moment's respite, to make myself a gold-mine? D'you

116

think I've crossed deserts and fought my way through jungles, all alone in my bed, to make a gold-mine? Look what my dreams have reduced me to! I look like a rumpled sheet! With all that dreaming, my existence has become a nightmare! While others were working in perfect safety, I was dreaming in peril of my life! I have slept without a moment's rest! I have slept passionately, to add something to the heritage of mankind! I have ransacked the night, I have risked my neck in the remotest corners of sleep, I have plunged into merciless labyrinths! I have dived head-first into dreams, fit to burst my lungs! And I've left some skin behind! My Sleepmaker is the fruit of an uncompromising imagination, it is the result of many years of strenuous sleeping!'

Joseph was shouting, his chest heaved and his eyes sparked fire.

'All ze zame . . .' said somebody.

It was von Schnopf. He fixed Joseph with a stern eye behind a thick monocle and went on: 'Zleep is zacred, von has no right to egzploit it for gommerzial entz . . .'

'Exploit sleep!' yelled Joseph, 'You must be out of your mind! My Sleepmaker will only cost fifty francs! Fifty francs for the privilege of sleeping soundly for the rest of your life, you call that exploitation?'

'And ze bublicity treamz?' von Schnopf persisted. 'Vot do you call zose?'

'The *what*? What the hell are you talking about?'

Binard intervened, intending to come to Joseph's defence. 'If Dr Cavalcanti's machine brings to consumers a high-quality sleep, there's no harm in incorporating a little advertising into it. Better a good sleep that includes a few commercial dreams than whole nights of insomnia! The future demands a new kind of sleep. A positive sleep, a young, athletic sleep! The sleep we practise today is no longer adapted to modern life, it has not evolved for millions of years, it's an archaic sleep, obsolete and completely out-of-date! In this era of computers and guided missiles, we are still sleeping like cavemen! Not only are people failing to produce

117

anything in their beds, they are not even consuming anything, either. Thus sleep turns them into economic invalids. Sleeping excludes them from society. We have no right to let things go on like this. Progress must include everybody! We must modernise sleep!'

Joseph had turned as white as a winding-sheet. His umbrella shook in his hand. He opened his mouth but could not articulate a single word.

Binard went on enthusiastically, 'If sleep is in trouble today, it's because there's no profit in it. But, thanks to oneiric advertising, that is about to change. The industrialists who invest in dreams, by buying advertising space in dreams, will have an interest in seeing that people will sleep well, whereas today, let's make no bones about it, insomnia is more lucrative than sleep. Soon, every one of our dreams will have a meaning and serve a purpose! Sleeping will be a contribution to progress! Sleep will at last emerge from the ghetto! It will become a profit-making product and form an integral part of the economic structure! We shall no longer sleep for nothing! We shall no longer sleep like animals! And all this, thanks to Dr Cavalcanti!'

At that moment, Joseph let out a yell, brandished his umbrella and brought it down on Binard's head, knocking him out cold. He fell like a log.

Next, Joseph hurled himself at von Schnopf and started shaking him as if he were a plum tree. 'I don't believe it!' he shouted. 'Tell me I'm dreaming, somebody, tell me I'm dreaming!'

Von Schnopf allowed himself to be shaken and rolled his eyes like a calf that's been taken to see *Murder in the Cathedral*.

Panting and distraught, Joseph made a clumsy attempt to stab his adversary in the belly with the point of his umbrella. Everyone rushed in to prevent him. He fell to the ground and began clawing at the parquet, the way he used to do as a child when they wanted to give him an injection. Foaming at the mouth, he cried out in a frenzy, '*Disgraziatu*! I want to go back down below! I want to go back! Put me in there, in the warm down below, down below, down below!'

8

It was a large white room with a half-open window and a fan whirring on the ceiling. Outside, the breeze was gently rocking the palms. In the distance, one could just glimpse a fragment of the ocean. An unknown bird, gilded and luminous, passed as if in slow motion across the blue chasm of the sky. Beneath the sheets, there was a rounded hump with a pair of feet on the end of it. 'This thing is me,' said Joseph to himself. It seemed to him quite preposterous that he should have a body. What an idiotic notion!

'*Comment allez-vous?*' enquired a voice.

Joseph turned his head. A man in an Indonesian-style blouse was sitting on a chair beside the bed. Joseph began to reflect on the question the man had put to him. '*Comment allez-vous?*' How are you going? In the first place, he wasn't going anywhere. As for knowing *how* . . . it's not as if there are dozens of different ways of going nowhere . . .

'Would you mind rephrasing that question, please,' he said, 'I don't understand.'

'I was asking if you're OK now,' said the other.

'*Urokaynow? Urokaynow?*' What the hell did that mean? Could it be the name of some divinity? Suddenly Joseph felt afraid. Perhaps he was dealing with a madman!

Then the man in the white blouse said, 'I'm Dr Ang Van Dong. I'm a psychiatrist.'

'Oh, really?' said Joseph. 'Well, I hope you'll get over it.'

The other man, immovable as marble, declared, 'You're still feeling the effects of the sedatives. You need plenty of rest.'

All at once, in a flash, the whole thing came back to Joseph.

'They want to put commercials into my Sleepmaker . . .'

'Yes,' said Van Dong, 'so they told me. Now don't worry your head about that.'

'Publicity dreams . . .' Joseph went on, gazing into the distance.

Down there, beyond the lukewarm city, beyond the sea, beyond everything, the sun was setting in a blazing silence. Above the bed, a beam of light illumined particles of dust in suspension, like planets whirling in the cosmos.

'Ah,' murmured Joseph, 'the dust is so lucky . . . Soon, I shall be sleeping an endless sleep, cradled by the rotation of the suns and the winds of space . . . Thank you, O God, for granting me nothingness, which is like a soft feather-pillow.' Then, turning towards Van Dong, 'D'you think they'll put advertisements into coffins one day?'

'Don't think about that,' replied the psychiatrist. He scratched the tip of his nose, cleared his throat and continued, 'I took the liberty of casting an eye over the notebook you had on you. You are certainly a remarkable personality, but you seem to be crushed by the weight of your mind. You should devote yourself to exercising your intelligence in a more balanced fashion. The fruits of thought carry within them the worm of anxiety.'

'Yes, ideas are hell. You think you're flying on Cloud Nine, and one fine day you realise you're crawling like a caterpillar. You think your head's a balloon that can lift you above it all, but you end up carrying it around like a millstone. Ah! How I envy simple creatures, people who know how *not* to ask themselves questions! Me, even when I'm taking a leak, I'm full of doubt . . . I'd have liked to be a peasant, get up at cock-crow and go out to wake up the rabbits . . . lead the chickens out to feed on the riverbank . . . milk the ewes in the shade of the pine-trees . . . I love animals, I'd have been good with cattle . . . Ah! Nature! . . . The wind in the trees . . . the water gurgling over the rocks!'

'Above all,' said Van Dong, 'you must moderate your dreams.

Your imagination raises you into states of exaltation that are harmful to you.'

'You're right!' exclaimed Joseph, his eyes shining. 'I'll never get excited again! I'll be a model of stern lucidity! The very image of clarity and precision! The torch of wisdom! The incarnation of pure reason!'

'Yes, yes, of course, but you must calm down. You must stop judging yourself by the yardstick of absolute values, measuring yourself on a cosmic scale. You're not a superman. You've pushed on too far with your rather hazardous experimental research, and . . .'

'I have pushed nothing too far, Dr Van Dong, all I've done is push the door ajar. A door which opens on to Wonderland . . .'

'That door opens on to nothing but a jungle. If you venture in, you're in danger of stepping on a lion's tail.'

'The state I'm in, fighting a lion would be a rest cure. A lion looks you in the face, breathes the air you breathe, and you can always come to an understanding with him. But That Which Has No Name . . . eh? For me, my bed is an arena in which, every night, I confront nameless horrors.'

'You're fighting your own chimeras. Breaking your teeth on your own dreams. Your nightmares are you. In my opinion, you should break out of your solitude. It's a bad counsellor. You need someone to stop you getting bogged down in your own thoughts. Even correct ideas can destroy us if there's nothing but a blank wall facing us. Being right, all on your own, is madness. As Kierkegaard said, "The door to happiness does not open inwards." You need something to attach you to the real world.'

'I've got my umbrella, that's all I need. Hey, where is my umbrella? And my clothes? I have to deliver my lecture . . .'

'Considering the state you're in, it's out of the question. In any case, it's too late. You've been asleep for twenty-four hours and the conference ends this evening.'

'What?' cried Joseph, leaping out of bed. 'Where are my clothes?'

'Where you can't get at them. You are in my care, Dr Cavalcanti, and it's quite impossible for me to let you out. Your mental equilibrium is at stake.'

'My mental equilibrium! But, don't you see, I'm the only one who's sane around here! Introducing commercials into sleep, isn't that insanity? Specialising in sleep-walking tortoises, isn't that insanity? Building supermarkets, parking lots and psychiatric hospitals in Tahiti, isn't that insanity. Men are going round the bend, they need me! Only sleep can wake them up! Don't you understand, they no longer know how to sleep? They no longer want to learn wisdom from their dreams, as our ancestors did, they don't believe in sleep any more! And when a man no longer knows how to dream, he loses all sense of reality. He makes himself a bed of oppression, injustice and barbarity! I must stop this happening!'

'Dr Cavalcanti, do you really believe men deserve all you're doing for them?'

'If I did nothing, I'd be the one who would be unworthy of being called a man, Dr Van Dong.'

The psychiatrist sighed and said, 'Now, you must look things in the face. This empire of sleep you dream about is a country that exists only in your mind. Each of us is alone in his own night. There are as many sleeps as there are sleepers. No communication is possible between dreamers.'

'And what if my dreams prove the contrary? Try to understand, Dr Van Dong: there are things one dreams about because they exist, and there are things which come to exist because one dreams about them.'

The psychiatrist scratched the tip of his nose and said, 'If you give your dreams the value they claim for themselves, you will never get out of them.'

'Whereas *you* will never get into them. A dream is not to be judged, it is to be dreamed, and that's that. You can analyse reality as much as you like while you're awake, but when it comes to dreams, wait until you're asleep to see them clearly.'

Joseph closed his eyes, overwhelmed by a profound lassitude.

After a moment, he went on, as if speaking to himself. 'Sleep is a deserted palace. The jungle encroaches upon it and mighty tigers prowl through it. They are the silent guardians of immobility. Awake, it's all very well to disdain these tigers, but who, in his sleep, would dare to pull their whiskers?'

'In any case, Dr Cavalcanti, I'm sure you'll find another opportunity of convincing humanity of the necessity of sleep. As for your dreams, I believe . . .'

'My dreams are none of your business,' said Joseph, abruptly re-opening his eyes. 'Keep your grubby hands off them!'

'As you wish. But in my opinion you must try to direct your psychic activity into other channels and invest your intellectual forces elsewhere than in sleep.'

'Direct your psychic activity into other channels and invest your intellectual forces elsewhere,' Joseph repeated, 'What sort of shopkeeper's gobbledygook is that? Really, one would think one was dreaming . . . and they say *I'm* the one who's mad!'

'Be that as it may,' continued the psychiatrist in a professionally optimistic tone, 'you already seem to me much better than yesterday! You'll see, the atmosphere of Tahiti will soon put you to rights. There are some sleeping pills in the drawer. Sweet dreams! See you tomorrow . . .'

'Dr Van Dong?'

'Yes?'

'I wanted to say . . .'

'What? Go on, I'm listening.'

'Well . . . er . . . you look a bit pale to me. I think I should examine you.'

Dr Ang Van Dong sat down at his desk and opened his medical files. With his tongue between his teeth, he meticulously traced CAVALCANTI JOSEPH in capital letters on a blank page and wrote the date of admission beside the name. Then, in a fine round hand, he wrote:

124

The subject presents all the symptoms of a classic paranoia with a tendency to psychasthenia, in Janet's sense of the word. He suffers from a severe failure to adapt to society and an incapacity for action that has led to a pathological over-valuation of his imagination. His apathetic-type megalomania leads him into an attempt to realise his fantasies of glory without ever leaving his bedroom. He feels he has been entrusted with a mission to send the whole of humanity to sleep, and that he is to be their leader. He wants to enthrone himself as the king of dreamland and rule over the universe from his bed. To this end, he has even invented a sort of sleep-inducing machine. When reality restores him to his senses, the shock will be violent. His aggressive impulses, if not turned inward against himself, could make him a dangerous individual. We must, therefore, envisage the possibility of a long confinement. I intend to keep him under observation for a few days and take the necessary steps to have him repatriated by the health authorities.

Satisfied, Dr Ang Van Dong closed his files. Then he stood up and took off his shirt. He would have to hurry to get to the stadium in time. This evening was to be the decisive encounter between the Wild Kangaroos, the football club from Sydney, and the Flying Postmen of the Tahitian G.P.O.

'Please God, let the knots hold!' Joseph murmured as he clung to the sheets and let himself slide down the wall. His private ward was only on the second floor, but he suffered from vertigo.

He closed his eyes during the descent and finally landed, safe and sound, in the grounds of the hospital.

He made his way towards the half-open main gate.

Nobody had noticed him, except an old Polynesian lunatic stretched out on a bench, but he appeared to be indifferent to the world.

Once outside, Joseph hesitated. He was wearing hospital pyjamas. His hotel was not far away but the Palais des Congrès was in the opposite direction. If he went back to the hotel to change, he would waste precious time and run the risk of arriving too late. '*Basta!*' he said to himself, 'There's nothing wrong with turning up in pyjamas for a conference on sleep. On the contrary, it'll show them I'm a serious sleeper.'

He therefore set out for the Palais des Congrès.

Now that he was walking, he felt the effect of the drugs more strongly. It was as if he were floating on air and his legs were moving all by themselves, like well-oiled machines. The palm trees, the cars, the hurrying Tahitians who watched him go by in his striped pyjamas and his slippers, all seemed far away and remote, lost on the moon. Only the sky seemed close to him, so close that he felt he could touch the crimson sun, scratch the flaming azure bowl and knead the unctuous golden dough of the sunset between his two hands.

He smiled at the passers-by in their colourful shirts, as if to apologise for looking down on them from such a height, for being so far above the world. Nevertheless, he perceived everything with extraordinary clarity: a woman's mocking smile, a child's navel, a dog scratching his fleas, a seagull perched on a palm-tree, some orange peel on the pavement . . .

He saw everything perfectly because nothing mattered to him any more.

Each detail revealed the entire universe.

Everything was essential.

A child chewing gum was as marvellous a phenomenon as the descent of the sun into the ocean.

He was no longer seeking anything, he wanted nothing, desired nothing and each object revealed itself to him as it really was.

No more past, no more future, he was a great, eternal Yes encompassing everything. And the innumerable No's surrounding him were annihilating themselves, putrefying on the spot.

His victory consisted precisely in having understood that there is nothing to be won.

He walked as if on cotton wool, detached from everything and yet, at the same time, bathed in reality as a fish is bathed in water. He felt fine, he was moving along on the current of life. Why worry about a thing? Soon all these people, who laughed as they saw him going by in pyjamas, would salute him as the Grand Master of Dreams, the Napoleon of Sleep. Thanks to him, they would one day be able to sleep with their heads held high, and they themselves would no longer be afraid to walk down the street in pyjamas.

And if nobody, ever, recognised what he had within him, if everything he had done was destined to nothingness . . . well, the same could be said of everything.

From the point of view of nothingness, Shakespeare is no greater nor more enduring than an ant.

The nothingness of everything would avenge him for everything.

He was walking down an avenue fringed with palms which ran along beside the beach. Beneath the luxuriant sky, the waves of the Pacific were so clear that he could see the silvery fish (in reality, they were plastic bottles). Behind him, the Tahitians burst out laughing. With a single word, he could have sent them back underground but he preferred to leave them to their stupidity. In his slippers, he marched on with the serenity of a conqueror, feeling magnanimous towards the mocking incomprehension of his fellows, to whom he wanted to offer the gold of dreams.

Only the dogs did not laugh.

Moreover, now and again, he exchanged a truthful look with someone, an old Polynesian woman or a drunk, whose eyes did not rest on his pyjamas but went straight to the innermost core of him, right through to his thwarted heart, where neglected treasures of goodness lay. And these poor people did not laugh either. Their looks, which suddenly illuminated him, like a shaft of love in his dark and lonely night, seemed to say, 'Courage! We can't do anything for you because life has crushed us, but we understand you, we are with you! Humanity is us!'

At last, he reached the Palais des Congrès. He entered with calm determination, walked down a corridor and entered the conference hall.

There was a speaker on the rostrum. '. . . for, at all times,' he was proclaiming, 'sleep has helped men to bear contemporary life! At all times, sleep . . .'

Mesmerised by the sight of Joseph advancing on him in pyjamas and slippers, the man stopped speaking.

A deathly hush had fallen upon the assembly. It was as if Christ, in flesh and blood, with the crown of thorns on his head, his hands pierced and his side lanced, had suddenly appeared in the midst of a synod of well-fed, gilded and ermined bishops.

All eyes were trained on Joseph as he made his way, without haste, to the platform.

At the foot of it, one of the organisers intervened. 'I am extremely sorry, monsieur, but, as you did not put your name down on the list of speakers . . .'

Joseph smiled at him indulgently and replied, 'I never put my name down anywhere.'

And with that he turned away, climbed sedately up the steps to the platform and approached the microphone.

The speaker, his face congested and his eyes goggling, stammered, 'Monsieur . . . who has authorised you to speak?'

Joseph looked into the whites of his eyes and declared calmly, 'I speak with the authority of dreams.'

The other man, in a fury, turned briskly on his heels and left the platform. With his chin high, he exclaimed, 'This is an act of pure violence!'

Joseph took his time. He let his eye run over this august assembly of eminent men of sleep, of doctors and scientific journalists, all of whom were uncertain what attitude to adopt. Can one listen with impunity, and without losing one's dignity, to a speaker wearing pyjamas? When in doubt, wait and see . . .

Amongst the audience, Joseph caught sight of Binard with a bandaged head and a grave look on his face.

Sitting beside him was Sonia.

Joseph was not in the least surprised to see her there. As an old campaigner of sleep, nothing could astonish him any more.

He scratched his chin (Damn! he'd forgotten to shave . . .), put his hands on the reading-desk, one either side of the microphone and . . . realised he had not got his lecture with him.

Never mind, no sweat, he had worked on it so intensively that he would surely be able to remember it . . . Let's see now . . . let's see . . . what was the opening sentence?

Every eye was fixed on him. The silence was nightmarish. Joseph made desperate efforts to recall his text but nothing came to him, nothing at all, not one minute morsel of a single phrase.

He felt all-powerful, all-seeing, all-knowing – and he had absolutely nothing to say. For once in his life, there was nothing in his head but a vast emptiness.

He shivered. He had nothing to say because he had nothing to say. He was facing a wall, a human wall full of ties and ready-made ideas, an impregnable wall of narrow-minded intellectualism, a wall studded with fashionable ideas and with prejudices as old as the world. He was facing honest and conscientious people, but people who might well take ten years to accept a piece of evidence from 'down below' although they would swallow instantly any bit of sophistry that came from 'on high'.

Like an eagle, Joseph bestrode the wind in an imperial silence. Words were far off, far away down there, like a swarm of ants squabbling over a few breadcrumbs. What was the good of speaking? If these people, at their age, still haven't understood, they never will. They are all specialists who see only what is under their microscopes, the rest of the world is shrouded in fog. Scientific flea-trainers. Choppers-up of molecules. Molesters of fruit-flies. And every one so stuffed with theories, so saturated with systems, theses and speculations, that it would be easier to get a fart out of a dead mule than to get them to change their concepts. They are too *well-cooked*. Done to death. Their brains have been boiled and re-boiled. Moreover, they eat nothing else . . . they will prefer a complex error of their own making to a truth that is common knowledge in the streets. They will always prefer the subtle exercise of their intelligence to the humble approval of a good, common-sense idea. They will always prefer a theory that takes up five hundred pages to an old proverb or the words of a simple man.

Standing like a ramrod in his pyjamas, Joseph had still not pronounced a single word. He looked like a perfect cretin, but that was because he was glimpsing the Absolute. Total clairvoyance gives one the look of an idiot. His silence prolonged itself cruelly, till he was sinking in an abyss of ridicule. But to explain anything at all to these super-subtle stick-in-the-muds seemed to him a waste of effort. For the truest things are the hardest of all for sophisticated minds to grasp. To understand the essential, one must not be too subtle, one cannot drink the living water that spurts from the rock with the elegant manners of the drawing-room. The organised stupidity arrayed before him sprang not from lack of intelligence but from an excess of intellect. It was stupidity caused by abusing the mind, it was a cancer of thought.

By now, the uncertainty of the members of the conference had given way to unease. Binard was smiling maliciously. Sonia had turned to ice. Joseph caught some pitying looks.

At last, through his elephantine lassitude, he managed to enunciate, 'What do you want me to say to you? You study sleep, I sleep. You would like me, perhaps, to trot out some new theory on sleep, like a conjuror pulling a white rabbit out of his hat? But the best theories make the worst nightmares. There's nothing to be said about sleep, it speaks perfectly well for itself. It is for sleep to judge us, gentlemen, not for us to judge sleep. First, sleep, then we will talk about it. Sleep can only be understood in bed, not at a conference. Endlessly discussing the why's and the wherefore's of sleep brings on sleepless nights. Sleep is a colossal mystery. Take advantage of this mystery, instead of

130

stalking it. Every night, sleep opens your eyes, yet you persist in dissecting it, slicing it up! But the night will come when sleep will avenge your pretentiousness. Your eyes will remain open, desperately open, and a fat lot of good that will do you! Beware of what you are about! Too much explaining turns you into imbeciles. Ever since we learned how to interpret dreams, we have had to make appointments with a specialist, spend a fortune and wait years and years to learn what a Papuan from New Guinea understands in the blink of an eye, because his mind is not distorted. Dreams, like works of art, are not to be explained, you can't interpret them, you have to feel them. But because their crudity disturbs us, because they shock our preconceived ideas, we close our eyes and cravenly set our reason to work so that we can label them and tuck them away into the right pigeon-hole in our overloaded brains. Then reason becomes intoxicated with its own cleverness. The more we make it labour, the more our intuition deserts us. So, if you please, leave sleep in peace! Put your reason away in the dog-kennel. If it needs to sharpen its teeth, give it a bone to gnaw, but leave it behind when you set out on the infinite steppes of sleep . . .'

Joseph adjusted the collar of his pyjamas, gripped the edge of the reading-desk like Christopher Columbus at the prow of his vessel and, with his nose into the wind (or rather, into the blast from the air-conditioners), he went on.

'When you try to find a meaning in sleep, you are like hens discussing the finer points of the slide-trombone. Sleep has no meaning. You don't sleep in order to rest, you sleep in order to sleep. Rest is no more than the indispensable complement of sleep. Sleep serves no purpose, but everything serves sleep. It is claimed that we need to sleep in order to live. But sleep is not a parenthesis in life, it is life itself, it is the very matrix of life. It is a black hole that absorbs everything and lets out not the faintest glimmer of light. It is not going anywhere, but everything is going to it. It has no meaning but gives meaning to everything . . . who can say whether sleep is not, in fact, our real life? For it is the

131

invisible target of all our acts. When one feels well, sleep comes. We are all drawn towards pleasure, and pleasure is the cool avenue bordered with sparkling fountains that leads to the enchanted palace of sleep. Perhaps we live to sleep, perhaps our waking life is nothing but a pretext for sleep . . . However it may be, all our miseries come from not knowing how to stay in our beds. If we accord sleep its true value, we will not be so greedy, nor so wicked. A good sleeper cannot be an evil bastard. Men who know how to sleep would be incapable of razing a forest to make an airport, or putting electronic fleas up a horse's arse, or transforming lakes into acid reservoirs, or of inventing more and more highly-perfected machines for slaughtering each other, or manufacturing toys that give children a taste for killing and destruction. But that's what we've come to: our society is in full production, turning out cripples of sleep. The interior life of these zombies, who are obsessed with their own egos, is reduced to working out their interest rates. They are the living dead, incapable of forgetting themselves, and therefore incapable of loving. Unable to love, or to be loved properly, they don't live any more, they just run their lives like a business. Having no faith in anything, they make a morbid cult of the self. They try to fill their inner nothingness by buying something – anything. Like Dante's damned souls, they try to lull their anxiety by a frenzied and aimless activity. They wriggle and squirm like fish in the net! The only people who escape this maelstrom are . . . the sleep-walkers. The apathetic souls who are addicted to tranquillisers, the amorphous ones, resigned and submissive, willing to dedicate their lives to somnolence so that, when they are lowered into the ground amongst the moles, they won't feel too disorientated.

'Meanwhile, what are you scientists busy doing? Murdering the mystery, introducing the worm of knowledge into the fruit of sleep, computerising life, canning reality and reducing the universe to figures so as to make them *accessible* and thus offer up the key to power, on a silver platter, to the butcher, the baker

132

and the candlestick-maker . . . Will you be satisfied, at last, when you've made the world square, when we can pop up to the moon to have a crap, when each fragment of reality is labelled and numbered, when everything has its exact name and its exact price? Let my mistake be a lesson to you! I, who today sleep in a state of war, I whose bed is an arena where, every night, there is a struggle to the death, I beg you not to hand over sleep, innocent sleep, to the businessmen! Save sleep! Spare it from your graphs, statistics, pills and electrodes! By making sleep an object of scientific study, you are behaving like kids who break their toys in order to find out how they work. Sleep is the goose that lays the golden egg. Don't shut it up in air-conditioned, aseptic, neon-lit poultry-houses – it will die! Respect the sleep that made you! Respect the hidden side of the mind! Leave man his night-side! Stop trampling all over Nature to improve her! Isn't this obstinate bias against Nature irrational and anti-scientific? The idea that everything which has not been modified by man is bad springs, surely, from the thinking of primitive magic. It is unworthy of science. The best is the enemy of the good. Trying to make things better at all costs, to make progress in the face of everything and against everything, without knowing where it's leading you, isn't that totally neurotic? Beware! Rationalise everything and you will beget madness! Do everything by numbers and you will end in barbarism! Reflect on these things. If progress exists for the sake of man, and not man for the sake of progress, how can you explain that a television set is worth more than a Peruvian child? Oh, I know one must not drift off into the blind cult of Nature. Nature is sometimes cruel. But she is cruel by accident, not systematically. To condemn nature for her occasional injustices would be like condemning sleep because of nightmares. Nature is not always good, but trying to improve her at all costs is always bad. Open your eyes and you will see that the essential part of scientific research is dedicated to struggling, not against the evils of Nature, but against the evils begotten by our so-called progress . . .

'Well now, Nature is not always good, but we will never make anything better than her. I assure you, we will never manufacture anything more perfect than sleep. No invention, no technology can make a man happier than when he's sleeping the sleep of the just. So, let us not trample on nature with the sole aim of accumulating knowledge that will explode in our faces. Good sense and truth have no need of giant universities, computerised libraries and international conferences. Let us beware of knowing too much, it is not the road to love, nor is it the road to liberty. Our ancestors understood nothing about sleep, but they slept well. In our cities at night, millions of men and women toss and turn under their rumpled sheets, sweating and haggard, waiting in anguish for the miracle of sleep. Ah! They would cheerfully give away their tellies and all their death-dealing gadgets to be able to sleep like dormice, little dormice snuggled up warm in their holes and sleeping like logs. Furry little dormice live without reason. We, thanks to our intelligence, will drop dead knowing the reason why . . . Oh, I can see you coming, you're about to accuse me of obscurantism, but don't you see that the worst scourges of our century are not in any way due to the last vestiges of barbarism, but to a surplus of reason? It is an exacerbated rationality that has begotten the techniques for manipulating the masses, multiplied the destructive power of weapons and set up the tentacular bureaucracies! Rationalism, by its very nature, tends towards totalitarianism. Whether this rationalism is ideological, administrative, scientific or mercantile, it is insatiable and, being incapable of self-limitation, it swells, encroaches, proliferates, crushes and gobbles up everything. And barbarity grows up in its shadow. Barbarity, gentlemen, is not the chant of primitive men dancing around their fires, barbarity is statistics. Figures are the ministers of death.'

Joseph took a second breath. For the moment, the words were coming to him so fast that he even had difficulty following them. Inspiration was pushing him out on to the open sea, towards an

134

unknown horizon. He did not know where he was going, but he was sailing gaily, the wind astern and all sail spread.

The delegates of the conference were looking at him with glazed eyes, like donkeys dozing in a field. Joseph, one finger raised and his eyes shining, went on enthusiastically:

'Gentlemen, sleep is not to be deciphered, it is to be slept. Sleep cannot be defined, it does the defining. Sleep cannot be weighed, it is the scales. Our society, sacrificing to the gods of efficiency, profitability and specialisation, transforms sleep into a vulgar physiological function, a simple means of repose. Thus sleep is no longer a pleasure, it has become a chore. One no longer *feels like* sleeping, one *wants* to sleep. Now, gentlemen, to sleep is the opposite of to want. One finds sleep because one is no longer looking for anything. The more you *want* sleep, the more it eludes you. The greatest enemy of sleep is the fear of insomnia, hanging over our beds like the sword of Damocles. We *must* sleep at all costs in order to get through the crazy treadmill of the next day. And so, we chase sleep away, for it does not obey our orders. It's not a dog, you can't whistle it up or call it to heel. The obligation to get up at a precise time prevents our having any carefree relationship with sleep, yet it is essential to make it our friend. (I am not speaking of the televisual torture we submit to every evening, which is to sleep what oil is to seabirds' feathers.) Limiting sleep to a particular span of time is like trying to put eternity into cans. Sleep must open onto the infinite, it must not be interrupted by the shrill ringing of an alarm clock.

'But, nowadays, instead of giving ourselves up to sleep, we consume it. Instead of retiring to bed with pleasure, we lie down in terror of not being able to sleep. Instead of opening ourselves to sleep, letting it send us head-over-heels into the depths of our innermost beings, into our intimate kingdom, we close our eyes with gritted teeth, as if we were being buried alive. By categorising sleep as a simple machine-like mechanism, we have turned it into a source of anxiety. Moral: when we attempt to control things too much, we become their slaves. Another moral:

our fear of the unforeseeable, of danger, of madness, of the misleading and the unknown, of disorganisation, drunkenness and the gratuitous, of poetry and love transforms our society into an ultra-modern breeding-centre for hormone-raised cattle with a built-in, press-button slaughterhouse.

'It is the fear of life that is killing us.

'You will say to me: at least we are free. Free to buy what we want, go where we like, say what we like. But what is this liberty that everybody seems to accept? What kind of freedom is it that makes everybody say, when faced with famine, war, the destruction of nature and all-pervading commercialism, "There's nothing we can do about it?" . . . Bah! A funny kind of freedom we have! We are free to go quickly or slowly, but only in the direction of the authorised arrows! We are free to decide which sauce we want to be eaten with! Free to choose the make of mattress and the colour of our sheets, but, night after night, we have to put up with the noise of traffic, aeroplanes and sirens! We are free to slave away for a whole year in the foul atmosphere of a factory to earn the privilege of spending a fortnight under the palm trees, twenty thousand kilometres away (because, at home, the forest is blighted, the river stinks of rotten eggs and even the birds have flown)! We are free to poison ourselves with sleeping tablets, but sleep, sweet sleep with its velvet paws and its tail in the shape of a question-mark, is fleeing our teeming cities like the plague!

'In truth, sleep is one of the basic rights of man, like silence, pure air, birdsong and fishing. But sleeping soundly is not enough. We must also sleep without haste, allow ourselves to be led wherever sleep wishes to take us. Those who sleep disdainfully, in bad faith, will not sleep far. A nightmare, with its hyena-like eye, will poke its stinking snout under their clammy sheets. For we cannot deceive sleep. It knows everything about us. It unmasks us. Forces us to turn out our pockets. Never let us forget, while we are so adroitly managing our petty existences from the tops of our heads, that sleep is managing us, putting us in our place, stifling our nights when, during the day, we stifle our own hearts. Each one of our little hypocrisies changes itself, at night, into an obscure beast that slavers over our faces. Sleep loves those who love, and freezes out the cold of heart. As for the lukewarm, he vomits them out. No, you can no more play tricks with sleep than you can with death.

'But our civilisation is founded on a denial of sleep and death. Just as we turn our backs on the world of dreams, so we conjure away our own death. That is why we labour like ants, idolising progress and the future. A progress that bears witness to our ineluctable decrepitude and a future that will see us under as sure as two and two make four. Would anyone agree to spend his days cloistered in an office, nailed to a typewriter, a telephone or a computer screen, cramming his head with figures and a thousand things that must not be forgotten, already dreading the evening rush-hour – would anyone accept all that if he was fully aware that he was destined to push up the daisies? No, gentlemen! When one knows how to look death in the face, one calmly cultivates one's garden with clear eyes and a light foot. Planting a tree, that makes sense in the face of death. Not being the servant of a machine in a factory or an office. To ignore death is to falsify life. The idea of death puts everything in its proper place, it consoles the good and obsesses the wicked, it gives to each thing its true savour and makes us love the best that life has to offer: silence, repose, forgetfulness, the mountains in their eternity, good wine, truthful books . . . and sleep. Far from making us passive, the consciousness of death gives us courage. What is there to fear, when you know that the worst is inevitable? Let us therefore accept Death at our table, let us feast and be merry with him, and when the time comes for us to accompany him to his mansion in the heart of the forest . . . well, we ourselves, well wined and dined, will take him by the hand, curious to find out where we are going. What a blessed journey in prospect! A transgalactic express, destination unknown . . . So, let us rejoice, gentlemen! The best thing in life is sleep, and the best thing in sleep is death.

'The fact is, no one can live like an egotistical rat and still accept his death serenely. Any more than one can lead a mindless, supercharged life and love sleep. Those who chase time will never find sleep. Nobody will ever be able to sleep on the *qui-vive* or on the run. Nobody will ever be able to sleep against the clock. Sleep does not know how to hurry. Its rhythm is not that of our computers, our factory-hooters and our traffic lights, it is the rhythm of the universe, the rhythm of the comets orbiting in the infinite night, the rhythm of the great All which beats in and around us. Gentlemen, I proclaim that by trying to conquer sleep you will find nothing but insomnia. If you plant the banner of science in the immemorial empire of dreams, you will transform it into an icy tundra. Or into a torrid desert inhabited by the ravaging locusts of insomnia.

'I am not speaking here as a poet. If we make a mockery of sleep, the reprisals could be beyond imagining. He who can no longer sleep can no longer think. Insomnia is a scourge. It stifles the defence mechanisms of the organism, just at this moment when every kind of aggression is multiplying. Viruses are also profiting from progress. They are propagating more and more rapidly and reaching further afield. They are becoming more and more virulent, more and more profitable. God help us if the ramparts of sleep should be breached and the horror creep out through the gap! Do not underestimate the danger! Let us open our eyes to the thing that threatens us, otherwise we shall never be able to sleep a wink! Let us not veil our faces with our so-called scientific integrity, that easy justification for our silence in the face of all the miseries of the world, for it is as if we abstained from declaring war on the dragon until we had counted all his scales. This stubborn refusal to take sides always benefits the party with the biggest teeth. And the circumspect, who take refuge in their seriousness, the wise and the prudent who remain dumb before the Beast or pretend they haven't seen him, are as culpable as those who caress him! And the Beast will devour them too! So, let us wake up and save sleep! Courage! Let us try to be a little less "experts" and a little more men! Let us fight the destroyers of sleep, the vendors of sleeping pills, the merchants of dreams and the public purveyors of sleep! Let us take up our swords, so that the sleep of the future – if there is one – will not become to true sleep what the hamburger is to our grand-mothers' pot-au-feu! Don't make a bed of insomnia! Half-sleeping is half-living! Without the joy of sleep, there is no more joy in living!'

Joseph spoke as if swept along on an interior torrent. His speech had absolutely nothing to do with the lecture he had laboured over so diligently, but he felt that it was the only thing he had to say now. He spoke without listening to his own voice, without forethought or ulterior motive, without rhetorical flourishes, without beating about the bush or sparing anyone, he spoke the words as they came to him and let them lead him wherever they would. He was no longer holding back, but gleefully taking the risk of saying anything whatsoever. He was improvising, as the nightingale improvises his song, as the sky improvises lightning and the dreamer improvises his dreams. His pyjamas lent him wings. When one is utterly ridiculous, one has nothing to fear. He was convinced that the entire auditorium was in the grip of his words. Admittedly, most of the members of the conference had begun chatting, or skimming through papers, while yawning their heads off, but is not true emotion always dissimulated under a mask of indifference?

Drunk on the wine that was flowing from him, flying on the wings of his own words, Joseph went on:

'Sleeping is putting one foot into the beyond, picnicking in eternity, gathering the daisies in paradise . . . All day long we knit and, at night, we play like cats with the ball of wool. At night, we unwind our spool, we unwind the bobbin of the universe . . . we are derailed amidst mountains of feathers . . . Sleep is right! It gives us nothing, but thank heavens for what it takes away from us! It restores us to ourselves. It dissolves our artificial *I* and gives us back our authentic *We*. For our true *I* is a *We*. Don't try to understand sleep, just listen to it . . . Sleep, O Great Interior of All that Is! Interior Elsewhere! Honey of Life! Sun of the night! Dance of the spirit! Sleep, the great helmsman, the king who rules over us all, who reveals all and effaces all! The masked sorcerer who grants us both the essential and the impossible! The kindly grandpa who takes us fishing for fabulous fish! The Uncle from America who comes back with his arms full of gifts! Metaphysical clown! Old wizard with the pointed hat, who knows us better than we know ourselves, who loves us better than we love ourselves! Sleep, great Sphinx! I bow down before your enigma, O you who respect my own mystery! You are the worst of vices and the pinnacle of virtue, the barrel of wine and the torrent of pure water, the brothel and the sanctuary! Sleep, you are the backside of the mind, the hidden face of life! You are the whorehouse of the angels and Dracula's kitchen, you are a harem full of cream cakes! Sleep! The Middle Kingdom! Fabled Cathay! The Queen of Sheba's palace! The library at Alexandria! Ali Baba's cave! The Court of Miracles! The secret garden! The Promised Land! Jerusalem the Golden! Babylon! Ocean into which the rivers of Time flow! Eternal carnival! Perpetual Christmas! Inexhaustible lucky dip! Mental trampoline! Wisdom of children and old men's box of toys! Mansion of the forgotten and mine of memories! Great Persian bazaar! Supernatural flea-market! Interstellar circus! Magic lottery with every number a winner! Pocket eternity! Free Luna Park! Forbidden granary! Treasure Island! Captain Nemo! Nothingness . . .'

Joseph froze, his arms outspread, his eyes turned up to heaven, offering his body to the divine light and waiting for the applause. But there came nothing more than murmurs of relief at the sight of two psychiatrists and a moustachioed policeman who, at that moment, made their appearance in the conference hall.

Joseph looked down at the organisers. When he saw their faces, stamped with pity and embarrassment, he understood.

Nobody had heard a word. The microphone had been switched off even before Joseph opened his mouth to speak.

If your name is not down on the list of speakers, you do not speak. Amen.

The psychiatrists were approaching calmly, followed by the moustachioed policeman, who seemed greatly intimidated at finding himself in such a place and among so many great and undoubtedly well-known scientists.

Joseph was livid.

Suddenly he started yelling at the top of his lungs (and this time everybody heard him).

'Callouskins! Callouskins! Callouskins!'

9

Stuffed full of tranquillisers, Joseph was repatriated by air. After a brief stay in a clinic, he was allowed home. He asked his concièrge to collect Livingstone and shut himself up in his dreamery.

He seemed to have aged ten years. For hours on end, he would sit sprawled in his chair with the cat on his lap. By day, he was taking anti-depressants, by night, sleeping pills. Not in order to sleep, but to avoid dreaming.

Several times he tried to get hold of Rapion by telephone, but he was always in a meeting, playing golf, gone to Pamplona or vanished to Timbuctoo. In any case, Joseph's hands were tied, the contract gave Rapion the right to carry out whatever modifications to the Sleepmaker he deemed necessary. As far as Joseph had been able to make out, Rapion intended to incorporate a radio into the Sleepmaker. Locked on a special wavelength, this would broadcast during the night some publicity spots conceived with the aim of provoking pleasant dreams. For example, they could create the sounds of a beach, evoking happy holidays, and associate this with the name, several times repeated, of any product they chose. It was as simple as ABC and, without the slightest doubt, diabolically effective.

Half-dazed by anxiolytics, Joseph had visions of financiers plundering sleep, he saw bulldozers clearing the jungle of dreams, steam-rollers spreading the tarmac of reason and profit throughout the land of dreams, he saw the ancient city of sleep filled with concrete tower-blocks, underground parking lots and giant shopping precincts . . .

He had played the Sorcerer's Apprentice, not knowing that it is easier to invent something than to master it once invented. He thought again of Christopher Columbus who, after defying men and the ocean, had offered America to the world. And then came the *conquistadores* who set about robbing the Indians in the name of God, forcing them to work like beasts of burden, organising slavery, sacking and despoiling nature with the sole aim of lining their pockets and riding in golden carriages. Christopher Columbus thought he had discovered paradise – and so he had; it was indeed an earthly paradise, but he did not realise that he had disembarked there as an emissary of the devil.

So Joseph buried his nose in the cat's fur and began to weep. Yes, sleep was paradise, and he himself had opened it up to greedy speculators.

He sank lower and lower. He was no longer living, he was dragging out an existence.

The mere idea of doing anything exhausted him. Washing a pair of socks became a Herculean labour. He felt he was carrying a rucksack full of stones on his back.

Perhaps it was his nature to do nothing, to watch the grass growing, to lie quietly and reflect on the meaning of things. He was not like other people. He must have a muscle somewhere that did not work. Action had always terrified him . . . but perhaps that was a trait of genius? Who knows whether Christopher Columbus conquered the New World simply because he was too lazy to run a shop? Or whether Napoleon became Emperor to escape from the fatigue of life in the barracks? Who knows whether genius is not the offspring of laziness? Who knows whether one reaches the zenith of thought to save oneself the trouble of getting off one's backside?

Anyway, what were they doing, all these busy-busy people in Paris? Spending their lives running around in circles, like horses in a circus, to earn themselves a nice juicy carrot!

Better to do nothing than work a treadmill in the void!

Each morning, at his window, Joseph was amazed at the cheerfulness of the deliverymen who, in spite of everything and as if unaware that existence is a tragedy, shouted vulgar witticisms at each other. And the sight of the postman, ringing at doorbells without a care in the world, brought tears to his eyes. What courage it took to deliver the mail every day and in all weathers, to say good morning to people and wear a cap! Joseph no longer knew how to get through life. His actions were all out of gear, he had spells of torpor when nothing could rouse him. He told himself that, at all costs, he must find something to believe in, a new reason for living. A reason external to himself. For to be one's own centre of gravity is fatal. Wanting to manage your life in your own best interests is spiritual suicide, a mental regression that inevitably leads you back to the larval state. For to live for oneself is to live for a future corpse.

Only . . . what to believe in, when everything seems specifically designed to disgust you, when you are driven into curling up inside your own shell, when the universal dogma is Every-man-for-himself? It takes more than one person to have faith . . .

One evening, Joseph took out his revolver. He could resign himself to doing without the things he desired, but . . . giving nothing to nobody? Impossible! So the only thing was to end it. Press the trigger and so goodnight. Afterwards, everything would take care of itself. Nothing more to be done. No choices, no decisions, no thoughts. Freedom, escape . . . To die is simply to dream for ever. Dream as the earth, water and clouds dream. To sleep. To sleep a little better, a little longer, a little more profoundly. We are not only our lives, we are also our nothingness, we are brothers to the stars, our atoms are the same as those of the most distant worlds. Death is not our enemy, she is our foster-sister. She is nature, as we are. Only those who live artificially, in falsehood and illusion need to dread

144

nature. But you . . . Nature loves you, you have nothing to fear. If you do not resist her, she will do you no harm. She will close your weary eyes just as, when you were in your cradle, she opened your eyelids onto life. Basically, it's all so simple. To die is to rejoin, at last, the nature you have aspired to, to rediscover what is essential, the essence of yourself that you share with the earth, flowers, animals and stars. Your soul.

Joseph remembered a proverb from his home town: 'It is better to be sitting than standing, better to be lying down than sitting, and better to be dead than lying down.' He loaded his revolver and looked out on to the street for one last time. A refuse lorry was passing by. A black dustman was running behind it, collecting the sacks with a feline grace and suppleness. 'He too is nature,' Joseph reflected, 'and he's alive . . . But what does he use all that strength and agility for? Collecting garbage. What would he think of me? I've never collected garbage. I don't do a hand's turn, yet I find life too heavy a burden . . . What a wretch I am, I don't deserve the air I breathe!'

He aimed the revolver at his temple. 'Come on, Joseph, just do it, get it over with. One little squeeze and *basta*! I can't say I haven't had a full life. Full of ideas, above all. And I dreamed well.' He composed an epitaph for himself:

> Here lies Joseph Cavalcanti,
> Who could not live except in sleep.
> If his poor memory you would honour,
> Kind passer-by, yawn long and deep.

Not bad. But he must also make a will. And make arrangements about the cat.

Discouraged, Joseph sighed and let his arm drop to his side. Even dying was a chore! Today, he did not feel quite up to it.

Shuffling in his slippered feet, he went and put the revolver back in the drawer.

*

In the morning, in bed, he tried to think of some valid reason for getting up. But not a glimmer of one could he find. To save the wallpaper, which the cat was meticulously tearing to ribbons? Right now, Joseph cared as much about the wallpaper as he did about what Julius Caesar had for breakfast. Then he told himself it was better to get up than to lie there trying to think of a reason for getting up. Once you are up, the reasons come. Even so, he did not always make it. The incentive was lacking, the divine spur that makes you act even if you have no reason for doing so.

'Suppose I write to Sonia?' he said to himself, while the cat, his pupils dilated with indignation, tore relentlessly at the wallpaper.

Since his catastrophic lecture in pyjamas, Joseph had been too ashamed to try to see the young woman. He had often tried to write to her, but his sentences always got out of control. They instantly transformed themselves into lamentations worthy of Job, or into furious imprecations against the entire world. The harder he tried, the more excessive his attitudes became. And he knew this would give people the excuse to rub his nose in it still harder. For, when a man is mad with misery, it is his madness others see, not his sorrow.

At the moment when Joseph ceased to debate the pro's and con's of getting up or staying in bed, he would finally get up without knowing why and, preceded by the excited cat, drag himself into the kitchen as if he had a ball and chain on his ankle.

Sometimes in the afternoons, to escape from himself a little, he would take his courage in both hands and go out.

One day, in a crowded bus, he found himself amongst some workmen who were coming home from work. They were harassed immigrants with crumpled faces and eyes like the eyes of beaten dogs. Their shoulders pressed heavily against him and made him feel almost well. It was not their sadness that comforted him, but the truthfulness of that sadness. Their suffering, which was neither false nor hypocritical, warmed his heart, whereas the affected well-being of the model consumers he saw in the more elegant districts, and the prefabricated optimism of the sporty types he saw jogging in their immaculate track-suits, froze his blood. For the space of a few minutes, he shared a human feeling with men who did not know how to hide or dissimulate anything, who had nothing to defend themselves with except their eyes. Several times he tried to recapture this simple sensation of human warmth, but it was difficult as he had to travel to the very outskirts of Paris and take himself into dodgy districts.

One day, at home, Joseph felt such acute exhaustion, such mental enfeeblement, so totally at the end of his tether that he lost his head and, succumbing to the ignoble temptation to obliterate his mind, went out and bought a television set.

During the days that followed, he set out methodically to turn himself into a zombie, sitting in front of the box of illusions and spinning his prayer-wheel.

He gorged himself on sport.

For him, sport had always been the apotheosis of the trivial, nonsense in action, modern absurdity in all its glory. But, suffering from a chronic lack of will, keeping going simply because it was the thing to do, with his backside like lead and his legs like toffee, Joseph was hypnotised by physical activity. The world of movement represented for him a paradise lost. Moreover, the spectacle of apparently-human beings devoting all their efforts to kicking an inflated bit of leather between two posts, while other beings, no less apparently-human, applauded them hysterically, seemed to him a greater mystery than the Immaculate Conception.

It was a vicious circle: the less he moved, the more agonising movement became, and the more anguished he became, the less he moved. He was wallowing in the glutinous quagmire of lethargy, he was being engulfed in himself. Sometimes, he would rather have died than get out of bed. However, he noticed that it was easier for him to perform some little chore for his cat than for himself. What he needed, then, was a bit of nudging. He thought nostalgically of his time in the army, when they kicked him out of bed with hob-nailed boots. In the barracks square, or at the controls of his tank, he had had no time to ask himself questions, and he had felt light, divinely light. The barking of the adjutant liberated him from his own mind. He had to march in step, not ponder on the meaning of things. And solidarity with his mates gave more salt to life than long, solitary meditations on the *Critique of Pure Reason*.

He dreamed, then, of enlisting in the Foreign Legion. But that would mean filling up endless forms.

Red tape was his *bête noire*. Applying to the Health Department for reimbursement of something or other was, to him, like cleaning out the Augean stables. Filling up a simple form, he felt his back was to the wall. Only when immersed in extraordinary ideas or impossible dreams did he feel at ease. He was not born to fill in forms, but to reach for the moon.

Just as happiness begets its own particular anxieties, so despair has its little pleasures. One learns to savour silence and darkness, the sound of the rain, the twilight hour . . . One becomes aware that real life is in small things and that any idea capable of ruining one's breakfast is, of its nature, false. Life is always here and now. The present instant is a sun, and all hopes of future happiness are dim candles in comparison. Going on from hope to hope, we arrive at the cemetery, but, in the heart of the moment, we find eternity.

Yes, despair has its positive side. It is sweet to lick one's wounds, snug and warm indoors, while the rain is pelting down and the other men are keeping their noses to the grindstone for mere peanuts. Pain is the best school for pleasure. It alone allows us to domesticate death.

Joseph understood that he should not struggle against his misery but settle into it as comfortably as possible. His pain was real, palpitating, rich, creative, so why should he coat it with a thin varnish which, in any case, would not stop him sinking into the depths? For you cannot vanquish your suffering by forced gaiety any more than you can cure warts with eau-de-Cologne. Pain is a form of energy. The energy of the soul. And it is fertile soil.

Thus Joseph was learning how to live again, coddled in his misery, curled up snugly in the depths of his distress. He swaddled himself in a closed universe, populated by his dear old books that told no lies. Having taken the precaution of pulverising his TV set with a blow from the prayer-wheel, so as not to be tempted any more by charlatans, showmen's patter and phoneys, he stayed at home, determined to have as little as possible to do with the greedy universal fairground, with its carrots-on-sticks, its murderous games and its exhibitions of freaks.

He made himself hot-water bottles, simmered tasty little dishes which he ate tête-à-tête with a decent bottle of wine and with the cat on his lap. In his solitude, he no longer said 'Poor me' but 'So much the worse for them'.

He began taking an interest in gastronomy, discovered that he had a talent for cooking and even put on a few kilos. And it was on a certain rainy evening in September, while making crêpes under the watchful eye of the cat, that he had his illumination.

He realised that the less the crêpe stuck to the pan, the better it was. The crêpe was life and he was the frying-pan. Not adhering to the things of life is the very condition required to savour them. Refraining from attaching oneself to the goodies of this world is not an act of virtue but the first principle of pleasure. The foreigner who travels through a country enjoys its beauty all the more because he knows he is only passing through. He is not seeking any kind of profit there, he can say what he thinks. Thus, carefree and disinterested, free as the wind, he sees people and things open themselves up to him.

149

To contemplate life with a pacified soul, to see it as a simple dream, is the only way to reach the heart of it. Is not the dreamer freer, more alive than the 'wage-earner' who clings anxiously to everything? To take your life seriously, isn't that to transform it into a nightmare?

While eating his crêpes, with bilberry jam, Joseph pursued his meditations. He understood that, the more desperately we cling to life, the more it eludes us. The more we cling to ourselves, the more lost we are. Hadn't Xenophon said that the most courageous warriors come out unharmed from the chaos of battle, while fear inevitably attracts the javelins of the enemy? Yes, the will to control your life rigidly, calculate everything, foresee everything, reduce the risks to a minimum so as not to miss out on anything whatsoever, fatally begets an existence dominated by frustration, anxiety and cowardice. The life of a hyena.

Joseph decided that life was only a dream and one should not turn it into a drama.

The fact that life was only a dream might discourage weaklings from undertaking any enterprise, but it stimulates strong spirits to dare all.

Joseph felt ready to dare all.

His pain was so profound that he no longer feared anything, and this sensation of absolute courage was very close to happiness.

He decided to elude Time.

Humanity had not wanted to follow him, well then, he would set off alone on the conquest of sleep.

Like the heretical monk who had fled the dungeons of the Inquisition in Toledo through sleep, he would try to escape from his miserable life by setting out on the perilous road of dreams. He would sleep without waking. He would sleep recklessly. He would sleep with one foot in the grave. He was ready to engage the Grand Inquisitor in single combat. If he succumbed, he would die heroically, in his bed, in the midst of a dream of glory. If he triumphed, the throne of sleep would be within his grasp.

Joseph threw his sleeping pills into the dustbin. Deprived of his Sleepmaker, which was in Rapion's hands, and already half-intoxicated by soporifics, he found it appallingly difficult to get to sleep.

Happily, he had more than one ace up his sleeve.

He found a joiner to make him a giant cradle whose rockers could be activated by the motor of a coffee-grinder. In this veritable vessel of sleep, he listened to old lullabies he had recorded, like the one his grandmother used to sing him:

> Sleep, sleep, sleep,
> Sleep is golden, sleep . . .

But in spite of all this, he found it impossible to shut an eye.

Then he started frantically counting sheep but, as a veteran of sleep, instead of going on like everybody else from one sheep to the next, he concentrated on a single sheep, then on a single hair of its fleece, then on a single atom of this hair until, at last, the atom bursting into millions of teeming stars, sleep carried him off on her wings.

Very soon he realised that, to evade Time successfully, he must find a way into the past. Find a secret passage leading to an earlier age.

He set a return to childhood as his goal. His destination was the world of fairy stories his mother used to read to him to lull him to sleep when he was small. On the walls of his dreamery he hung reproductions of Gustave Doré's poignant illustrations to Perrault's tales, which he re-read every evening with a sorrowful heart. It was there, in this forest full of magic spells, where one cannot take ten steps without getting lost and every word is a secret formula, and where the enchanted palace of the Sleeping Beauty lies shrouded in a bluish mist, that he would find his lost paradise.

But to sleep so far, he needed Ariadne's thread. He went down to the cellar, rummaged in all the corners and at last discovered what he was looking for: his old school satchel, which had accompanied him throughout his childhood and adolescence. Opening it, he breathed in the ashes of his youth. It smelled of ink and dead leaves.

That evening, Joseph went to bed with his nose in his old satchel, determined to sleep to the death. Further down, as if more deeply buried in the satchel, there was the smell of his infancy. But it was first of all his adolescence that came back to mind.

He remembered . . .

His lycée was right beside a zoo, at the top of a cliff that looked down on the station. From his desk by the window, near the radiator, he had watched the trains departing, thousands of trains, for years and years . . .

It must be noted that, far from being a recent passion, sleep had always been a veritable vocation for Joseph. His youth was punctuated by two incessant *Leitmotifs*: '*Not up yet!*' from his parents and '*Always asleep!*' from his teachers.

In every class there is a tough, a clown and a sleeper. Joseph was the sleepy-head of his class. The sluggard, the good-for-nothing, the incorrigible idler, the king of the day-dreamers, the prince of dunces, the object of his teachers' pity and contempt. The gymnastics master, in particular, prophesied for him a future of idleness and failure. If these people had been obliged to point out the disgrace of the class, a scapegoat for all the ills of the world, a victim to be immolated or sent to the galleys, they would unanimously, without a shadow of a doubt, have chosen Joseph Cavalcanti. However, while the other pupils, their heads stuffed with silly popular songs, dreamed of nothing but girls' bottoms and motor-bikes, he was asking himself why he had been born. In his case, desire was not a joke, it was a torment. Love was not a game, it was a mortal combat. He did not even have a girl-friend. As he watched the trains departing, he was obsessed by an idea, constantly reiterated: 'In an unknown town, there lives an unknown girl. We were made for each other but we shall never meet. We would have loved each other, but we shall die without ever having seen each other . . .'

It was with this memory on his mind that he fell asleep, hugging his old satchel. But he had only overheated, foggy and truncated dreams, the dreams of a rank amateur.

For three nights, he soldiered on. His sleep was like a vast beach where broken dreams, the flotsam of his past, were washed up and stranded.

Nevertheless, he felt that, in his sleep, he was surveying the ground, preparing for take-off. Then he was on his way.

On the fourth night, he strayed into the future.

He found himself in a magnificent city with streets lined with palm trees, and pavements covered in broadloom carpet. The people, young and dynamic, glowed with health and enjoyment of life. The women were very beautiful, everyone was smiling. Joseph went into a park. On a bench at the edge of a small lake, the old Chinese antiquarian was sitting, knitting a sock. Joseph went up to him and said, 'Well, still old, are you?'

'Ah, yes,' replied the other, sighing. 'And you, still asleep?'

'Always. But I don't feel sleepy.'

'That's normal, you're dreaming.'

Joseph sat down on the bench. 'When all is said and done,' he remarked, 'humanity is well out of it.'

'Yes,' said the old Chinaman, 'well out of it because there's nobody left.'

'What do you mean, nobody left?' said Joseph, turning to look at the people who were strolling through the park and greeting each other with the words 'Everything's fine!'

'Oh them! It's only their bodies. Their brains are in tins, *down there below.*'

Joseph woke up feeling sick.

On the fifth night, he at last dreamed of a street that led into the past.

On the sixth, he started down the road but had not the courage to continue.

On the seventh night, he went down to the end of the street and entered the past.

153

Carrying his satchel, he was walking down an avenue lined with plane-trees whose trunks were covered with announcements. A knife-grinder was pushing his little hand-cart. An itinerant glazier, his back bent under a load of glass panes, was shouting: 'Gla . . . aaa . . . aaasss-mender!   Gla . . . aaa . . . aaasss-mender!' A housewife with a bun on top of her head was carrying a block of ice in a string bag. Near a public urinal, girls with long plaits, pink dresses and white shoes, were playing hopscotch on the pavement; others were playing with hoops or skipping as they solemnly chanted mysterious incantations.

It was the old days and Joseph knew it. But all the others seemed unaware that the time would come when they would belong to the mists of the past, when they would be nothing more than vague phantoms of days gone by, faint recollections straying through memories that were themselves destined to become dust. And Joseph was seized with nostalgia when he saw these young girls who would become ancestors, these passers-by from the past who would disappear one day, like the old Citroëns and 202s that were backfiring on the cobblestones.

Joseph knew he was asleep and that anything was permissible: he could piss into a cart, nick a cream cake from a pastrycook's, break a few jars in the chemist's shop, pinch the bottom of a passing girl or trip up a coalman bent under his sack . . . He could abuse his own dream, do anything he liked. Only he did nothing, because, as usual, he was late. He had to run. All out of breath, he at last reached the lycée. Avoiding the scornful eye of the concièrge, he dashed up the stairs.

When he came into his classroom, there was a general shout of laughter – he had forgotten to dress, and was still in his pyjamas. He stammered his excuses and, shamefaced, went to his desk under the stern gaze of the mathematics master who, as it happened, was The Father of the People dressed in white overalls. Joseph sat down at his desk near the window. He put on

154

an alert expression so as not to attract attention, while The Father of the People began to discourse:

'Gentlemen,' he declared in solemn tones, 'mathematics is part of the prestigious and distinguished family of things which serve no purpose, like butterflies, the galaxies and pyjama bottoms. When, in the course of your existence, you come across something which serves no purpose, do not spit on the ground nor turn your eyes away with a grimace of disdain! On the contrary, raise your hat to it, for you can be certain that this thing has never done anyone any harm and never will. Without things that serve no purpose, life would not be worth much.'

Joseph looked out of the window. It was night-time, the sky was swarming with stars. In the distance, he could see the outline of the byzantine cathedral and the funnel of a steamer. A crescent moon was reflected in the inky sea. A ship's siren shrilled, then he heard the roar of a tiger. Below, in the station, the steam engine of the Orient Express was spitting out a plume of smoke. The train was about to leave. 'If I hurry,' said Joseph to himself, 'I could still catch it . . .'

'Are you dreaming, Cavalcanti?' said The Father of the People. 'Always looking at the trains, aren't you? You remind me of a certain ruminant, famous for his interest in railways, but whose name I will not repeat out of respect for the lady director of this establishment.'

Joseph sighed and forced himself to pay attention.

'Now then,' continued The Father of the People, 'that which serves no purpose is always a source of joy. Mathematics is no exception to this sacred rule. Anyone who fails to burst out laughing when faced with an equation of the second degree is a patent ass, incapable of grasping the comical nature of the universe, sublimely characterised by the rich absurdity of the mathematical sciences!'

Joseph saw one of the pupils eating a book. He remembered that he was dreaming. Soon he would wake up and be back in his grey and monotonous life. He would once more be strait-jacketed into reality and the present.

Down there, the Orient Express, glittering with lights, was about to pull out . . .

To depart! To depart! This train was the dreamed-of opportunity never to wake up again! To flee far, far away, into Childhood, into the Orient of sleep!

Stealthily, inch by inch, Joseph slithered down under his desk. There he found a trapdoor. He opened it, slipped beneath it and, leaving the classroom unseen and unheard, began to descend a spiral staircase.

The stairs became steeper and steeper, narrower and narrower, the treads were made of rickety and worm-eaten wood. Joseph's steps faltered more and more, the hand-rail gave way, his descent became a fall . . .

The staircase turned into a toboggan, Joseph shot swiftly into darkness . . .

He clutched his cock and, using it as a hand-brake, pressed it as far as he could into his stomach.

He managed to stop just in time, on the platform.

It was deserted. Not a soul in sight. Under the immense glass dome of the station, a clock indicated an impossible, aberrant hour, a time outside time, outside numbers, outside everything. Joseph thought that this hour must belong not to time but to the female of time.

The train was on the point of departure. All the doors were closed.

A loudspeaker announced, *'Will all dream-without-return passengers travelling to the castle of the Sleeping Beauty please board the train at once . . .'*

At this moment, Sonia appeared at the window of a compartment. She was dressed as a Russian countess with a fur toque on her head.

Joseph flung himself at the door, but he could not open it. He shouted, 'Open the door! I want to go with you, I don't want to wake up again! I want to go to Childhood, all the way down there, just after China!'

156

Sonia neither heard nor saw him. She was looking fixedly ahead of her, with glazed eyes.

Abruptly, the train jerked forward and began to slide out alongside the platform. It left the station, carrying the indifferent face of the young woman into the depths of sleep.

In distress, Joseph watched the last carriage disappear. And then, at the end of the platform, he saw the Grand Inquisitor.

His face was as white as a shroud and his black robe like the darkness of the tomb. In his hand he held a frying-pan.

Mad with fear, Joseph rushed into an underground passage.

He ran, ran like the wind, not daring to look back.

Finally, he reached the foot of a monumental staircase.

He called out, 'Is there anyone there?'

The deathly silence that followed was worse than the most terrible reply.

Joseph began climbing the steps.

Little by little, the staircase was transforming itself into an ordinary staircase in a house. Joseph's legs grew heavier. He looked at his hands: they were all wrinkled. The hands of a ninety-year-old.

He was old, his feet felt like lead. But still he kept climbing, without rhyme or reason.

At last, he found himself in front of a door. He opened it and stepped into a room that reeked of dust and darkness. He caught his nose in a spider's web. The room smelled like the mysterious granary. It smelled of the freshness of olden times. It smelled like when he was a small boy.

In the middle of the room stood a chest. A toy-chest. *His* toy-chest.

Deeply moved, he went over and opened it. All his toys were there. The miniature cars, the building set, the Zorro dressing-up outfit, the fire engine, the clockwork bird, the water-pistol . . . All his toys. They had not aged . . .

With tears in his eyes, Joseph took his Teddy Bear in his trembling, old man's hands and embraced him and pressed him

157

against his face. Then he went over to a window which let in a trickle of light. He pressed his nose to the glass and looked out. On the opposite side of the courtyard he recognised the window of his dreamery and saw himself lying in his bed, asleep.

Then he heard footsteps climbing the stairs. The footsteps of the Grand Inquisitor.

Joseph would have given all the gold of sleep to wake up, to find himself safely in his bed. But one cannot wake up to order any more than one can go to sleep to order.

The footsteps had reached the landing. The door creaked. Joseph, his teeth chattering, dived into the toy-chest like a rabbit into its burrow and covered his head with everything that came to hand. Then, arms crossed and a rigid smile on his lips, he froze in the attitude of a doll. He had only to pretend to be a doll, then nobody would do him any harm.

Above him, large hands began rifling through the chest. Joseph, the smile petrified on his face and his heart a lump of ice, heard a sugary voice saying, 'I smell the blood of a living man . . .'

Joseph realised he was committed to a deadly game of hide-and-seek with the Big Bad Wolf. He wanted to cry out, 'Pax! Let's play some other game!' but the Big Bad Wolf was not playing.

Joseph stopped breathing. Fear gripped his entrails. Suddenly a rasping finger touched his face and he heard, 'Toys don't have noses, I know that . . . and toys don't have ears . . .'

'But I'm a doll,' wailed Joseph, 'I've a perfect right to a nose and ears.'

'Dolls don't have moist lips,' said the Grand Inquisitor, 'dolls don't have beating hearts . . .'

'It's not me in here,' protested Joseph.

'Ugh! The naughty little manny tells me he's not in there!'

'You won't hurty-wurty little me, will you?' squeaked Joseph, paralysed with fright.

He could not see the Grand Inquisitor but he could feel his big calloused hands groping for his body under the toys.

'Ooh, the little rascal,' the representive of the Holy Office went on in a honeyed voice, 'he's ventured a little too far into sleep, he's lost in a dream and now he's hiding . . . he knows that's not nice . . . he knows he's going to be punished . . . he knows I have a big pair of scissors . . .'

At that instant, Joseph heard the sharp click of a pair of scissors. The Grand Inquisitor began to chant in the tone of a priest elevating the Host:

> 'I cut off all to make amends
> Even little dangling ends . . .
> A-a-a-amen . . .'

Seized with panic, Joseph began burrowing down through the toys. He dug and dug, like a hysterical mole . . .

He found himself in a vast cavern full of giant toys. The lead soldiers were as big as he was and the rocking-horse the size of a real horse. Joseph forced his way between huge red and yellow building blocks and glass marbles as big as balloons. He noticed, without emotion, that he was no longer old.

He put on the mask of Zorro. The Grand Inquisitor was lurking somewhere, disguised as a lead soldier or a fluffy bunny. The Grand Inquisitor could be any one of the toys. Joseph hesitated between giving himself up in the hope of attenuating the severity of his punishment, and running away.

He decided to play the Invisible Man and therefore started walking in the way one usually walks when invisible.

Suddenly he stepped on one of his old school exercise-books. He picked it up. Written in clumsy letters on a white label were the words:

CAVALCANTI JOSEPH
Dream Notebook

He opened it and read:

RECIPE FOR DISAPPEARING WITHOUT TRACE AND REAPPEARING WITHOUT MAKING BUBBLES

Arm yourself with a really sensible head and a good mirror.
Look at your head in the mirror.
Shut your eyes and think intensely about what you have just seen.
When you have a clear picture of your head in your head, stop thinking without warning.
If you have done everything correctly, you will have disappeared.
To reappear, open your eyes slowly.

Joseph started hunting for a mirror, but in vain.
He leafed through the notebook and read:

RECIPE FOR FINDING A SUITABLE MIRROR
Arm yourself with a pair of knitting needles.

Damn, he didn't have any knitting needles. Ah! Just what he needed:

RECIPE FOR FINDING A PAIR OF KNITTING NEEDLES

At that moment, he heard a horrible clicking of knitting needles, accompanied by the voice of the Grand Inquisitor chanting:

   'A needle is the best of toys
   For poking holes in naughty boys . . .
   A-a-a-amen . . .'

Horrified, Joseph decamped at the double.

After an endless odyssey through sweating passages and cellars full of plumbing-pipes and spiders' webs, Joseph found himself in the basement of the Natural History Museum. He climbed a staircase strewn with fragments of old bones and came out into the hall of the tyrannosaurus. At the end of the room stood a gigantic organ. A triangular clock indicated a frightful hour of the night.

160

'Night rhymes with fright,' said Joseph to himself.

Beyond the windows, he recognised the blue forest that surrounds the castle of the Sleeping Beauty, the tenebrous forest where Tom Thumb got lost. In a dusty old baroque mirror, with an over-ornate frame, he saw himself going by, wearing striped pyjamas and a necklace of flowers. His face was the haggard mask of an old wolf of dreams.

He did the rounds of the showcases, where the skeletons of illustrious palaeontologists, in frock coats and top-hats, were displayed. In one corner of the room stood a stuffed curator.

Joseph went up to the tyrannosaurus. With the air of a connoisseur, and as if to persuade himself that he was used to doing it and there was no risk, he stroked the reptilian tail.

'So, still loafing about in sleep?' said a voice behind him.

Joseph whipped round. An icy chill ran through him. It was the Grand Inquisitor.

He had the face of Fernandel.

He was wearing a gilded bishop's mitre and the white apron of a pork butcher. His mouth was split in a wide horsy grin. He was holding a woodcutter's axe in one hand.

Still smiling, he went on in a cut-glass accent, 'I say, you young scoundrel, you're sleeping between very fine sheets, aren't you? Sheets that smell confoundedly of pine, like a coffin! Eh what, you young rascal?'

The Grand Inquisitor then took Joseph's dream notebook out of his pocket, opened it and declared, pulling a face at the same time, 'None too brilliant any of this, what? . . . Let's see if you can give me three words that rhyme with "red" . . .'

Rigid with terror, Joseph could not utter a word.

'Bed . . . ' the Grand Inquisitor resumed, 'bed, dread, dead! I'll have to give you a nought, a jolly big round nought.'

Joseph, half-choking, managed to stammer, 'You can't do anything to me because I'm dreaming.'

The Grand Inquisitor replied icily, 'Do I look like a face in a dream?'

'No, of course not. I didn't mean to offend you. But I beg you to take into consideration the fact that I stand before you merely in the role of a sleeper. After all, at this moment I'm in my bed, sleeping. I'm even sleeping very soundly. I'm having a little nightmare, that's all, it can happen to anybody. But it's only a matter of time till I wake up.'

The Grand Inquisitor sneered: 'Time? Here? I wouldn't count on it if I were you.'

'I know, I know, but sooner or later all bad things come to an end. Don't they?'

Without deigning to reply, the Grand Inquisitor began humming as he nonchalantly dusted off the blade of his axe:

> 'Loitering in your bed
> Is not what you were made for.
> Naughty children know
> Their dreams must all be paid for . . .'

Joseph would have given his right arm to be wide awake, anchored to reality and concrete things, with his head on his shoulders and his feet on the ground. But you can't get out of a nightmare just by doing a pirouette. The cup must be drained to the dregs.

Meanwhile, as a wily old fox of sleep, Joseph knew that nothing is more dangerous than fear. To believe you are at risk is to run a great risk. In sleep, as in all things, it is wise to be bold. And never let yourself be intimidated by objects, such as a wood-cutter's axe. He therefore declared diplomatically, and in a matter-of-fact voice, 'I must confess I have strayed somewhat from the beaten track of sleep. I have slept with immoderate enthusiasm. I have dreamed with excessive curiosity. But it was all done without ulterior motives. I am ready to wake up as soon as you like.'

'Here,' said the Grand Inquisitor, 'there is no waking up.'

'Listen, sleep is big enough for both of us. We could come to an arrangement . . . I'm very good at making crêpes . . .'

'You don't deserve your sleep,' replied the Grand Inquisitor. 'You have soiled dreams, you have tried to make money out of the wings of angels, you have tried to harness dreams to the miserable wagon of materialism!'

'As God is my witness, I never wanted that! My Sleepmaker could be of benefit to everyone.'

'Things that benefit everyone benefit first and foremost the profiteers. You have opened the ivory portals of sleep to carpet-salesmen, and now you want to sleep like a pig to forget your crime! You want to take root in your bed, you want to make your nest in sleep! But you cannot elude Time. Sleep is a gift of life, not an escape-hatch from reality. He who flees by sleep will perish by sleep. For the peace that oblivion brings is not peace. The freedom that forgetfulness brings is not freedom. Shame on you, dreamer of hell! You deserve to be smothered between two mattresses, like a mad dog! A mad dog of laziness! You are nothing but a foot-dragging sluggard! A thumb-twiddler, a squashed slug, who reigns from his bed with a pillow instead of a sceptre! Ah, I'll make you lose your taste for dreaming, you idle wearer of slippers! You Napoleon of the bed-sheets!' Then, pointing to the tyrannosaurus, he went on, 'If somebody trod on his tail, he didn't take refuge in sleep!'

Joseph saw the axe glinting above his head. He stepped aside hastily – the blade swished through the air, two centimetres from his ear. Enraged, he grabbed a prehistoric umbrella from one of the display-stands.

The Father of the People, who was sitting at the organ wearing a Louis XV wig and costume, started playing a funeral toccata. The Grand Inquisitor, brandishing his axe, began to sing in a tenor voice:

> 'Dear child, you'll do better without your head,
> You'll be much more relaxed
> Once you've been axed
> And chopped up small to make my bread.'

The axe whirled in front of Joseph, who parried the blows as well as he could with his umbrella.

'I'm in my bed, in my bed,' he kept repeating to himself as he recoiled before the furious onslaught of his enemy's axe. But this famous bed was as inaccessible to him as the treasure of the Incas, and the battle raged on round the fossil tyrannosaurus while The Father of the People, at the keyboard of the giant organ, indulged in some hallucinatory improvisations.

Meanwhile, little by little, Joseph was beginning to retaliate boldly, fighting tooth and nail, striking out vigorously, displaying some fine cut and thrust with his umbrella, so that now he was a real danger to his enemy, whose frenzied axe whistled about his ears.

Joseph had nothing to lose. He had his back to the wall and, curiously, he felt fine. For once, he was letting himself go. He was letting himself go and determined never again to let himself be put upon. At last he had before him a true adversary, someone who hated him, someone for whom he counted, instead of one of those human chameleons who specialise in hypocrisy and subterfuge, those experts in bad faith who people the waking world and over whom he had no power whatsoever.

But suddenly, with a ferocious blow of the axe, the Grand Inquisitor cut right through Joseph's umbrella.

Once again the axe whirled and plunged down at him. He leaped back. Too late. The blade gashed his chest.

Howling with pain, he threw himself on the ground to dodge a third blow. But now he was at the mercy of his enemy, who brutally put his foot on his stomach.

Then, raising the axe ceremoniously, as if it were an Episcopal cross, the Grand Inquisitor intoned a canticle:

> 'He sought for fame and glory
> By sleeping like the dead,
> But now he'd give his right arm
> To wake up safe in bed.'

Joseph was quaking in every limb. With a Fernandelian grin, the representative of the Holy Office stared into the whites of his eyes, chanting, 'Now the gentleman with the big axe is going to chop off the heady-peddy of the naughty little boy . . .'

And he closed one eye, the better to aim.

'Have some respect for the pyjamas I'm wearing!' Joseph implored. 'Grant me a stay of execution! I'll buy back my soul, I swear it by all the saints of sleep!'

'And you will write out one hundred times: I am a little slug who never learns his lessons . . .'

'Yes, yes, yes, I promise!'

'Good. Well, just this once, I'll spare you the axe. But instead . . . instead . . .'

'No!' yelped Joseph. 'Not that! Have mercy! Not tickling . . . not tickling. . . !'

And he woke up laughing his head off.

10

'Ah! At last, here's one all on its own!' Joseph exclaimed, his eyes glued to his binoculars.

He got back into the hired deux-chevaux, which he had carefully covered with branches, drove off and headed down the track of the military zone in the wake of the tank.

He had hyped himself up. He had drunk half a litre of black coffee laced with cognac.

With his hands gripping the steering-wheel, his jaws clenched, his eyes bloodshot and his backside suffering from the jolting of the infernal old rattletrap, he stamped on the accelerator.

A few minutes later, the camouflaged 2CV came to a halt in a little thicket, where it lay in ambush. The tank was coming, sending up a great cloud of dust. It was a creaky old Sherman, dented and rusty and, judging from the state of the armour-plating, it must have been used for target practice. Joseph smiled. If this was really the case, they would undoubtedly have detailed the skivers and dunderheads of the regiment to drive it. The same thing had happened to him during his time in the army. He remembered the purgatorial hours he had spent crating up plaster shells in the dust and heat of overheated steel, in a temperature of 50 degrees. Enough to drive you bonkers.

The tank, all unsuspecting, approached. Joseph pressed the accelerator and the 2CV emerged from the thicket, wobbling and jerking, to block the tank's path. The big armoured vehicle, with its caterpillar-tracks jammed, stopped within a hair's-breadth of the car, accompanied by a fearsome grinding noise.

A chubby and mortally indignant face popped out of the turret.

''Ere! You can't do that!' shouted the soldier, while Joseph climbed out of the little car. 'Cor, you won't 'alf cop it if they catch you! They'll flatten you out like a bleedin' pancake! Are you sick or summink? Civvies ain't allowed on this road, it's military, it's forbidden! Can't you read the notices, mate? You nuts or summink?'

'I'm extremely sorry,' said Joseph, 'But I must ask you to get out of that tank.'

'What?! Are you out of your tiny mind? And, in the first place, mate, 'ave you got a permit to drive round 'ere?'

'No, I've just got this.'

And he pulled out his revolver.

'Come on, out of it!' he said. 'Out! And move your arse!'

At that moment, he heard a clucking from inside the tank. The chubby soldier, suddenly as pink as a prawn, got down from the turret. After him, another soldier climbed out of the tank, holding two chickens up by the claws, one in each hand, and looking extremely foolish.

'Are there just the two of you in there?' asked Joseph.

'Well, yeah . . .' said the chubby soldier. 'Two plus the chickens . . . 'Cos we've got chickens, see?' And he showed them to Joseph, as if he might not yet have seen them. 'We didn't mean no 'arm . . . We was taking a stroll, see, near your farm, and they come towards us, all on their own, like . . . In't that right, George?'

'That's the livin' truth,' confirmed the other, still holding the chickens, which were clucking hysterically and flapping their wings.

'Ah! You see, I'm not telling no lies! As I was sayin', they fell in love wiv us at first sight. We couldn't abandon 'em, poor buggers, now could we? And besides, we're defendin' our country, we've got a right to a few fresh eggs! But, since they're yours, OK, they're yours. George, give the gentleman back 'is birds! Shall we put 'em in the car for you?'

'Fuck the chickens,' said Joseph, who was having the time of his life, 'what I want is the tank.'

'Huh? The. . . ? You've got a screw loose, mate! It's droppin' to bits, this bleedin' machine, you won't even get a nail out of it! It still goes, Gawd alone knows why, but it's just a 'eap of scrap iron 'eld together wiv elbow grease! And what are we goin' to tell them back at the barracks? We've miked off wivout permission as it is, if you pinch our tank on top of that, Christ, they'll 'ave our guts for garters!'

Joseph replied, 'You'll tell them that, having heard a suspicious clucking, you took the initiative and made a reconnaissance, during which you were attacked by a 2CV.'

'Oh, shit! I joined up to 'ave a nice quiet life, and now I get assaulted in the bleedin' woods!'

'I'll leave you the car,' said Joseph. 'There's some cognac in it.'

'Cognac?' said the chubby soldier, his face lighting up.

Joseph, leaving the two soldiers standing there, climbed quickly into the tank. Amidst a cloud of floating feathers, he sat down in the driver's seat and strapped himself in. The old reflexes came back to him, he put it in first gear, locked the left-hand caterpillar track and accelerated, causing the tank to pivot on its own axis. Then he set out along the road that led out of the military zone.

He looked at the fuel-gauge and pulled a face. He would have to requisition two or three hundred litres of diesel from a gas station. He could just picture the pump-attendant's face. Moreover, it was Saturday morning, the sun was shining and people were hurrying out into the country. He could hardly pass unnoticed on the main road. Well, tough luck, at least he was sure of finding his man at the golf-course. But first, he wanted to make a tour of the sleeping-pill factory, with a view to finding out how solid the walls were.

11

The ball hesitated for an instant on the rim of the hole. Then, as if
sickened by this life without hope, by all these silly buggers in
checked trousers whose idea of relaxation was to beat hell out of
the ball (as if they were trying to drive their bad consciences as
far away as possible), it decided to topple over into the hole.

'Magnificent putt, sir!' exclaimed Adolphe, Felix Rapion's
chauffeur-cum-bodyguard.

His boss, after making a superhuman effort to restrain himself
from jumping into the air and howling with joy, replied with truly
British phlegm, 'I'm improving, Adolphe, I'm improving,' then he
added, 'I'm sure I did the right thing, buying the best clubs.'

'Certainly, sir,' said the chauffeur-cum-bodyguard, who knew
his man, 'it's not money down the drain. These clubs are superb,
they're made to last a hundred years.'

Felix Rapion suddenly felt uneasy at the thought that the golf
club he was holding would outlast him. It would still exist, some
idiot would still be holding it in his paws when Rapion was six feet
under, trying to sell sleeping pills to the moles . . . Yet surely his
life was worth more than a golf club – a whole lifetime of effort and
vexations, with the telephone, the urgent appointments, the
files, the taxes, the trade unions, the business suits that chafcd
his skin . . . all that, but it would not enable him to escape the
worst: he would go down into the hole, like the golf ball. So what
use was it, all that aggravation? What was the purpose of this life
of trouble and anxiety, this race against the clock, since it led to
nothingness and oblivion? To provide bread for his family? His

family? His family . . . a wife whose life was poisoned by the feeling that she was no use to anybody, children brutalised by the telly . . . The little one, at thirteen, was already dressing like a . . . No! Better not to think about that. God knows, he was paying enough for his relaxation. But, every time he unwound, it was the same thing: gloomy ideas came into his head. As if the birds and the trees were calling him to order, reminding him, in chorus, that one fine day the sun would rise without him and he would be lowered into the ground between four planks.

'Would you like a wood for your next drive, sir?'

'A wood? Er . . . no, Adolphe, not for the moment, I must get my concentration back first,' Felix Rapion replied to his chauffeur-cum-bodyguard, who also served as caddie, to save extra expense.

In fact, he would have liked to savour his victory before going on to the next hole, but Adolphe's tactless remark about the club had really put him down. He breathed deeply, determined to feel well if it killed him. Besides, there was no reason why he should not feel well. Business was going great guns. There was so much money to be made everywhere that he hardly knew which way to turn. For fear of missing something, he was thrashing about like a demon in a stoup of holy water, he no longer had a moment to himself. He had almost had to give up his golf, but that would have been a strategic error. Golf was part of his image, his trademark, and it was on the green that his most sublime ideas came to him, such as that of the advertising Sleepmaker. Golf was his spiritual nourishment. The green spaces and the pure air recharged his batteries. The time he spent here was not money wasted, no, sir! On the green, his spirits rose, he saw the world at his feet, like the ball he hit with such grace and power. Like a solitary eagle, he dominated this barbarous world, he soared above the common herd, he was a free man, free, free, free . . . as free as the peasant he had seen on the telly, in the commercial for *reblochon* cheese.

'It's true,' he said to himself, 'that I toil like a soul in hell, I have to be everywhere at once and supervise everybody, but I make money, and money is freedom. When you can purchase the means to do nothing, it's well worth the effort of driving yourself hard! Ah, life is beautiful! There are so many things to buy! And so many things to sell!'

He turned towards his chauffeur-cum-caddie, who was also his confidant, and declared with an assumed jovial air, 'A bit of nature does you good, doesn't it, Adolphe?'

'Certainly, sir. Here, you hardly feel the pollution, and you don't hear nearly so many planes as you do at your factory.'

'Say *our* factory, Adolphe. Yes, yes, it's very important to me. We all form one big family dedicated to the noble cause of sleep.'

As he spoke these words, he turned towards his factory, which could be seen some two or three kilometres away, between the airport and the dormitory town called The Blue Forest. He could even encompass within his gaze the homes of his employees: the modest tower blocks of the workers near the factory and the more elegant housing estates of the engineers, built a little further away to escape the stink of rotten fish that emanated from it. While playing golf, Felix Rapion liked to contemplate his enterprise, although his pleasure was always a little tempered by the fear that some maladroit pilot would crash a 'plane on it. But, today, it was something else that disturbed him.

'Tell me, Adolphe . . .'

'Yes, sir?'

'It sounds ridiculous, but I . . . um . . . I have the impression that my . . . that our factory is not the same shape as usual. It looks to me . . . how can I put it? . . . Flatter . . .'

'It's the sun, sir, it flattens the forms. It's just an optical illusion, known to many artists.'

'Ah, is it? A trick of the light? All the same, I'd like to be quite sure, just to set my mind at rest. Have you got your binoculars?'

'They're in the car, sir.'

'Very well, go and – But, Adolphe, my car . . .'

171

'What's the matter, sir? It's down there on the golf-club parking lot.'

'But . . . but, doesn't it seem to you a bit . . . flattened?'

'Flattened, your Mercedes? Certainly not, sir. It's the reflection of the light that gives it that squashed look.'

'Really?'

'No need to worry, sir. But perhaps it would be wiser if you were to go home now, sir. You didn't bring your cap, and the September sun is treacherous.'

'Yes, you're right, Adolphe.'

What an idiot he was! Worrying himself to death over a simple optical illusion! But he was so sensitive, so emotional . . . Suddenly he pulled a face. His pain had come back. Right, this time there would be no more shilly-shallying, he would go to a doctor. A good doctor, a serious and competent man, a specialist capable of reassuring him completely, even if it cost a packet.

The air was suddenly torn by a rumbling sound above his head. He raised his eyes. An aeroplane was circling in the dirty blue sky.

'Look, Adolphe!' he exclaimed. 'It's a twin-engined executive jet! I've ordered the same model, it'll be delivered next week! It's beautiful, isn't it?'

'A superb machine, sir.'

'Perhaps that one's mine, they told me they were going to carry out a few tests.'

Like a virgin in ecstasy, he watched the 'plane. But suddenly his face clouded again.

'Adolphe, don't you think it's making a peculiar noise, that aircraft? A . . . a sort of rattle . . .'

'It's not the 'plane making that noise, sir, it's coming from behind the bunker . . .'

'It is?'

He cocked his ear and, in fact, he heard a sound like a load of scrap iron grinding and clanking. The green beneath his feet began to quake. Suddenly he saw a sort of long metal tube appearing from behind the bunker, and then a grey mass that looked like the turret of –

'Good God!' he cried, his eyes out on stalks, 'a tank! On a golf-course! No, really, that's insufferable! Do something, Adolphe, don't just stand there like a – '

But, beside him now, there was no Adolphe. He had melted away like butter on a hot spit. There was nothing but the golf clubs scattered over the grass. Adolphe was already in the far distance, running like a hare.

'This is insufferable,' repeated Felix Rapion more quietly, his voice half-strangled, as he saw the back end of his chauffeur-cum-bodyguard-cum-caddie-cum-confidant disappearing over the horizon.

He turned back towards the tank. The steel monster, grinding, snorting and farting, was advancing on him, slowly but surely. For one second, Felix Rapion allowed himself to believe it was a nightmare. It felt like a nightmare, after all, and it tasted like one.

But it was no nightmare.

Felix Rapion's face crumpled. As far as he knew, he had no enemies other than the Tax Inspector. He remembered now that he had put all his golfing equipment down as business expenses . . .

Nearer and nearer crawled the giant caterpillar. He was about to be crushed like a snail. Distraught, with his golf club still in his hand, he searched for a tree to climb, a hole to throw himself into. But nowhere was there a tree high enough or a hole deep enough.

'Mama!' he bleated, taking to his heels.

Behind him, the tank accelerated with a roar.

Epilogue

My dear Sonia,
When you see the island on the blue horizon, it looks more like a dream of the sea than a real island. Once you disembark, you realise that, apart from the sky, nothing is to be found in abundance. There is only one specimen of each object.

It's quite something even to find a road that leads to a simple grave under an oak tree.

Perhaps this little cabin is the refuge of some wise old man, and this stone, in the shadow of some ruins, the resting-place of a familiar ghost.

A moss-covered roof, a donkey rolling on the grass, a deeper silence without apparent cause, a lizard lying in wait for the breath of a flower, a butterfly with crepuscular wings perched on the rim of a well – all this is nothing, but it is irreplaceable. And these little nothings give meaning and purpose to everything.

A strange country, a stranger to itself, where the sempiternal old women know the secrets of the Beyond better than they know the next village.

Here, there is not much activity. Time is empty. Clocks are a rarity and often they're not going, anyway. The figures are back to front, the hands bent or missing. At the station, the railwayman took the trouble to get a ladder and climb up to the clock, which had stopped. Not to put it right, but to cover the face with some adhesive tape, so as to make it clear that this arbitrarily-arrested moment of time was a mistake, and that the true time was . . . er, well . . . you'd have to look elsewhere for that.

177

I admired this effort, not to reactivate a mechanism, but to sanctify its immobility. An eminently spiritual undertaking, profoundly humane, which does credit to the loyal employees of the SNCF.

What good is time? Nothing is ever worth the trouble of hurrying. Here, asking the time is frowned upon, and hurrying as unseemly as, in Paris, delaying half a second before putting your foot down when the lights turn green. To be in a hurry shows that you do not understand the art of living. The old folks say that thinking about time shortens your life.

The main occupation of the day is looking for a shady spot. Here, shadows are places. Havens of rest where one can settle down peacefully with a minimum of fuss. Each shady spot has its own particular quality of coolness. Finding the best shade is the gift of wise men and cats.

Did you know that a tree should be valued according to the quality of its shade? In this country, you could almost say that things are little more than a pretext for the shade they give.

The old men, sitting in the café with their walking-sticks between their knees, watch the universe go by. It is easier for them to see into the heart of things than to lift their little fingers. Living is learning to do nothing. And they possess this supreme art, making of their idleness something sublime. Blessed people, who know that their slow pace is the road to eternity, that the gods can only be encountered when one is calm in body and mind, and that it is in the heart of repose that one must seek the mystery!

I must add that, if nothing is urgent, it is because nothing is undertaken lightly. The slightest yawn is pregnant with consequence.

People live poised for the beyond, as if each gesture were destined to vibrate for ever, like a chord on the guitar resounding through eternity.

In this country, death is no stranger. In death, you are still at home. Even more at home. So, nobody tries to evade death. And death is in no hurry to arrive.

178

There are graves everywhere. Down there, under the cypress, and in front of the shop where you buy bottled gas, and again, opposite the bus stop. The point is, the dead have no reason to hide themselves away. Nobody is ashamed of being dead. On the contrary, it gives one a certain prestige. Here, to be dead is an honour, a luxury one flaunts before the unfortunate living, who are obliged to get up every morning. Yes, nothingness is a privilege, and, for the rest, you will see nothing but phantoms in their Sunday best.

> Like sleep, death must be deserved.
> Death is the sleep of sleep.

Last night, I dreamed you were getting married to Binard, that miserable microbe I knocked out in Tahiti. If such an abomination were to occur, I should have only two alternatives: either to blow my brains out, because imagining the woman I love soiled by a performing dog, picturing beauty between the paws of a tail-wagging mongrel, would be more than I could bear, or to laugh so hard that I fell on my backside. Undoubtedly, I would choose the second solution. Since I touched rock-bottom, I laugh as often as I yawn. Besides, one should take love tragically but never seriously. Be that as it may, I am sure you possess a soul and you would never grant the unworthy Binard the ignoble pleasure of sullying it.

Talking of souls, I have bought mine back. The papers called it 'an act of insane fury on the part of an inventor who felt he had been swindled'. All I did was go to Rapion's factory at the controls of an assault tank and, with all the care of a conscientious housewife doing her ironing, flatten the laboratory where they kept the prototype of my Sleepmaker. While I was at it, I also demolished the factory; it was an eyesore on the landscape. Then I went to the Chantevaux golf club to settle the hash of that unspeakable swine, Rapion. I had every intention of squashing him into the ground, but he made me laugh too much. When I saw him scampering off in his plus-fours, so fast that his feet never touched the ground, then flinging himself into a pond and floundering about amongst the frogs, with his wallet between his teeth and a water-lily on his head, all my hatred gave way to hilarity. Besides, I could see from his congested face that he is not long for this world. So, I left him to himself which, all things considered, is the worst punishment anyone could inflict on him.

After these escapades, I went and gave myself up to the head-shrinkers. They shut me up in a very pleasant asylum in the country, where I met some charming people. I already knew that I got on well with children, animals and drunks, but I did not know that this would hold good for nutcases, too. The company of lunatics has somewhat reconciled me to the human race. As long as there are madmen, all is not lost. Of course, you can't put all loonies into the same basket. Some of them have gone mad from too much rationality, but a lot are mad out of an excess of life. Like high-flying sleepers and comedians, the insane let their minds run riot, they let them drift with the current and flutter wherever the wind chooses to blow them, carefree and without ties. This freedom brings them no profit, they do not acquire any of those easily-broken toys the majority of men sweat blood to get, but it is a pleasure in itself, perhaps the essential pleasure of life. Sonia my dear, may you be blessed in the name of sleep, laughter and madness, the Holy Trinity that nourishes our souls, raises us above the dandelions, and allows the flowers in paradise to breathe!

After five months in the psychiatric hospital, they pronounced me cured and authorised my release back into the anthill. I had to pay Rapion every penny I had. After that, my cat and I decided to pack our traps and come back to my home, to my village. We've been here for several weeks now. He is in fine fettle, farting firecrackers and, as for myself, I am recovering, little by little, by taking the hair of the dog.

My warrior-like exploit has earned me a certain prestige. In Paris, I didn't count for much, but here I am almost a Somebody. They call me the moon-doctor.

In these backward countries, insomnia is an unknown disease. The people can be divided into two categories: those who have just got up and those who are just off to bed. The priest and the village chemist being the only insomniacs, my visits are limited to people who are worried about sleeping too much. In the evenings, I am often invited to supper, as they like to hear me talking about Paris. As I sit in the chimney-corner, eating *bruccio* washed down with wine from the plain, I describe the traffic jams, the people who talk to themselves in the street, the metro at rush hour, the frenzy to buy things, and all that glaucous aquarium, full of over-stimulated fish, where the water's never changed. *A merda in ochju è u focu in culu*, as the old boys comment, laughing heartily as they peel the hot chestnuts.

Ah, there's nothing like a good laugh to make you sleep well!

Here, people laugh, eat, drink, tell stories, hunt boar with great pomp, take siestas and leave nature in peace. Amongst the industrialised nations, the grass is fouled with bitumen and the stars are hidden in smog. Here, there's still grass beneath your feet and stars above your head.

Certainly, everything in this country is scarce, except the grass and the stars. A few things, a few words, surrounded by sea and sky. But it's so much better this way. It seems to me that quantity fuels anxiety. Numbers suck our blood like vampires, masses suck our souls dry, too much is never enough. In the big cities, there is a lack of emptiness, of dead seasons, of areas of shade, and of ghosts. Everything serves a purpose, which gives one the feeling that one is nothing but a hyphen between objects. Nothing but a fragment of solitude in the midst of a blind mass. If you only knew how much better you feel when you are not pressured by all the multitude of things you have to do, to see and say! And, in any case, there are different forms of profusion here. Meanness is not the strong point of the locals. Elsewhere, you are proud of your possessions, here, you are proud of what you give away. To be lavish in giving with a casual air, that is the salt of life, the luxury of luxuries, almost worth risking damnation for.

Hoarding up the pennies is looked upon as degrading. With such a mentality, you may say, these people won't go far. But they don't need to go anywhere, they've already arrived. They appreciate their pleasure far too much to wear themselves out running after pleasures. Since effort has to be followed by rest, they prefer to get the rest in first.

I have come to understand here that true happiness, like spring water, has no taste. True happiness cannot be felt, it is in no way palpable, it is the absence of trouble and worry. It is a void, a pure cloudless sky, a sleep without dreams.

I have also come to understand that one is never happy because of the things one has acquired, but because of the things one has avoided. For example, my dreams have not brought me a thing, but they have spared me a great deal.

If it is not within my power to achieve the glory of a Napoleon, why shouldn't I be as happy as a rabbit who runs over the hills, sits dreaming at the edge of fields and, deep in his burrow, sleeps more soundly than an Emperor? One should compare one's destiny to that of simple people, to birds and trees, and not to the fate of mankind's heroes, for, that way, you build your own private hell. Personally, failure has taught me to find a taste of honey in the land. Fame? *Basta*! A man who cannot bear obscurity could not bear glory, any more than a man who does not know how to savour the present could be happy if he were given all the treasures of King Solomon. Besides, glory and repose have never walked hand-in-hand. And obscurity protects you.

My cat, Livingstone, shares my opinion. He sits for hours, crouching in front of mouse-holes, teaching me patience and the sensual pleasure of silence and the delight of being hidden. For him, this place is paradise. He feels no desire to reign over it because he is fine as he is.

In the end, perhaps all the things that happened to me were due to the fact that I slept badly.

I've changed my mattress.

By the way, what would you say to getting out of the goldfish

bowl and coming to visit me? There are no night-clubs in my
village but there are stars in the sky. The shade is so soft and the
earth so rich that to be dead would seem almost a pleasure. This
is the ideal country for sleeping. And there's everything you need
for doing nothing: secret springs, mysterious paths, deep
shadows, old haunted ruins, a silence that seems to come from
the very depths of time, and then good wine, goat's-milk cheese
and nice crusty bread. You cannot imagine how much you can
learn just watching a donkey grazing in a meadow, nor how
soothing sheep are. The song of the nightingale will wake you up
in the middle of the night to make you savour your sleep all the
better, then he will sing you gently back to sleep. In the tall
forests, you will have the time and space to walk at your own
pace. Your cares will be carried away on the current of the
stream, and the wind that blows through the chestnut-trees will
blow away your gloomy thoughts. The mountains will exalt your
ideas, the distant sea will cradle your day-dreams.

I am ashamed of having ignored the birds for so long. I believe
that the true direction of life is in the drawing nearer to nature,
and to your own nature. Thus, growing older is not a decline but a
rising up, and dying is not an end but a crowning event.

Yet it is not enough to love nature, one must protect it from
those who are destroying it. For this paradise of ours is under a
terrible threat. But, *basta*! I am waiting for you with all my love,

Joseph

Sitting on the bank of the rushing stream, his chest bare and his
feet in the water, Joseph folded up the letter and put it in his
pocket. The cat, with his whiskers quivering in the breeze, was
perched above him on a branch that hung over the foaming
eddies.

Joseph leaned over to look at his reflection in the water.

Dreamily, he contemplated the deep scar that furrowed his chest.

The cat yawned majestically.